About the author

Paradise is Carol Ann Cole's fifth book and her first work of fiction. She is a best-selling author, professional speaker and the founder of The Comfort Heart Initiative.

Carol Ann is a member of the Order of Canada, and has received numerous additional awards including: Queen Elizabeth 11 Silver and Golden Jubilee Medals, the elite Maclean's Honour Role, the Bell Canada Heroes award, the Markham Stouffville Hospital Hope award and the Terry Fox Citation of Honour. She is profiled in *Canadian Who's Who* and in the 2005 edition of *1000 Great Women of the 21st Century*.

You can contact Carol Ann directly at www.carolanncole.com

She would love to hear from you.

For Demi

PARADISE

team

♥

love
Caroll...

Carol Ann Cole

PARADISE

Vanguard Press

A CIP catalogue record for this title is
available from the British Library.

ISBN 978 1 784652 24 1

*Vanguard Press is an imprint of
Pegasus Elliot MacKenzie Publishers Ltd.*
www.pegasuspublishers.com

First Published in 2017

**Vanguard Press
Sheraton House Castle Park
Cambridge England**

Printed & Bound in Great Britain

Also by the same author

Comfort Heart – A Personal Memoir (with A Kapoor)

Lessons Learned – Upside the Head

If I Knew Then What I Know Now

From the Heart – The Ripple Effect of the Comfort Heart

Acknowledgements

Paradise is a work of fiction with a hint of reality. Cape St Mary is real. Carol and Russ, Anna and Bobby, Benoit, Tanya, Debbie, Anna and Ed, Yvonne and Robert are a few who have answered my questions regarding the fishing industry, and the Cape. Thank you so much for your help.

Aurèl and Andrée Comeau, thank you for giving me permission to write about your house on Cape St Mary Road and to have a likeness of the house I fell in love with on the back cover of *Paradise*. Phyllis Pedicelli, thanks to you for the beautiful sketch.

Connie Dea, thank you for your proofreading, your edits and so much more.

To my son, James Scott, thank you for listening – always.

Thank you to Mary McCann for helping me understand life as a nun. I appreciate your letter full of facts and personal experiences. It was extremely helpful.

To photographer John Carvalho, thank you for all photos used in promotional material for *Paradise*.

Finally, thank you to Claire-Rose Charlton, Production Coordinator, Pegasus, and to others on the Pegasus Elliot MacKenzie team who have worked with me. I hope we have a long and successful future together.

For James

Prologue – 1972

I've made my decision. I choose him. My wardrobe might include 'the sexy red one' after all.

No, wait a minute, I've made my decision. I choose Him. The screaming match inside my head is finally over. I'm relieved to hear the sound of silence. Until now, it's been impossible to make such a huge decision and stick with it. Time is running out and I'm rationalized out too. Suddenly there might be someone else to consider. Someone more important than anyone – including me. Twenty-some hours to zero hour.

This time it feels different. It feels right.

Only Wilmot, my brother, knows exactly where I'll be. He knows about the other decision I've reached as well. He's begged me to change my mind – to let him *help me*. He, naively I think, believes Mom and Dad can help too. I know what *must* be done and I will *not* change my mind.

Wilmot has promised to keep my secret. Forever. I trust him with my life. With our lives.

Bless me, Father, for I have sinned…

Part One

The Paradise Journals

1

1967

Today is my eleventh birthday. Mom gave me a diary and honestly I have wanted one since I was little. I'm going to write my whole life story here. I'll go through all of my scribblers and decide what's important enough to be copied. I might not write every day because some days my life is so boring I could just die. Waiting for some excitement around here seems to take forever.

In my scribbler-diaries I've been writing about my name for years. My name is the biggest problem I have. Who calls their daughter Paradise? I have a few good friends and when I talk to them about my name they're nice and they understand why I wish I had a different name. But my other so-called friends laugh at me behind my back. They laugh at my name and they laugh when I tell them what I'm going to do with my life.

My middle initial is d. My parents won't tell me what the d stands for. They just keep saying, "It is 'd' in lower case, Paradise. Someday we'll sit down and tell you everything. You'll know the story behind the letter when and if you must." All I want to know is what the *d* stands for. I don't want a lecture. Is that too much to ask?

And what does *if you must* mean?

***

I plan to journal every damn day. Actually I want to stop swearing so this is a good place to start – I plan to journal every day not every damn day. I may slip up but I'll try to stop swearing. I hope I have at least a few secrets to write about, as I get older. I don't have many right now. To be honest I have *none*.

This isn't really a secret but my Sunday school classes are the best.

I really like my summer catechism classes too. They last for six beeee-u-ti-ful weeks. Every catechism class prepares me for my calling. *I'm going to be a nun.* When the time is right I think God gives me a new name so… problem solved.

Paradise nobody will become Sister somebody.

It's true my name is a problem but honestly I'm happy most of the time. I love, love, love my brother. Wilmot is five years older and he's really good to me. He's a bit dull if you know what I mean but maybe that happens to boys as they age. I don't know. Mom says I'm old for my age and my brother is young for his age. I don't know what that means either.

We live in a nice apartment and my mother is all about cleaning and cleaning some more. She uses the spit polisher to put paste wax on the living room floor every time someone is coming over. There isn't any spitting involved but that's what we call it. I think Mom likes using the spit polisher even when company isn't in *the plan*. Dad always says, "So what's in the plan for this weekend?" and Mom tells him if someone is coming to visit. Mom is in charge of all the inviting.

Mom makes me happy. "Where is that spit polisher when I need it?" I laugh every time I hear Mom say that.

Our concierge in our lobby is my friend. *He knows my name.* "Hello, Missy Paradise. Don't you look fetching today." We can't call him our concierge when we're talking to other people because Dad thinks we sound highfalutin' when we call him that. Whatever.

***

My First Communion happened years ago. I have replayed that Sunday over and over by gently placing a raisin on my tongue pretending my parish priest is standing in front of me giving me my Holy Host. A raisin is the best I can do. One rainy day (when I was a kid actually) my brother snuck up behind me and threatened to tell my secret if I didn't turn my pack of raisins over to him. I didn't receive my Holy Host at home for a whole three weeks until I saved up enough money to replace my raisin stash. Wilmot and I laughed about it later but at the time I was pretty sure I hated him. That didn't last long because he apologized and gave me a few extra boxes of raisins as a please-forgive-me-gift.

***

I'm back.

I plan to write every day but months have gone by so I decided I better sit down and get busy with more of my life story. Mom says I need a routine.

Even before now I've been very carefully writing down the teachings of the Catholic Church. This stuff is preparing me for my life when I finish school. Some of these learnings still take lots of time for my mind to understand, so I write them down and study them while other kids my age are outside playing stupid games.

When I enter the convent I will be a postulant and that word means my first year in the Order. Then as a novice I think I will kind of be on probation. My brother was on probation once but Mom and Dad would never tell me why. I don't think it had very much to do with the church.

I have read about the Grand Silence. 'Keep your mouth shut between seven p.m. and seven a.m.' That's one long stretch of quiet.

I forget what it's called but I know another requirement is to keep my eyes lowered so I don't see anything that will distract me from God. Like Thomas next door who is even cuter than Elvis Presley. I call this the Keeper of the Eyes and I practise all the time – eyes down, eyes down, eyes down every time I see him. I'll write more about my Thomas later. (I only call him *my* Thomas when I write his name down.)

At some point wanna-be-nuns have to maintain a whole *year* of silence while they think about the life they have chosen. My plan is to get rid of that rule before my turn comes.

Mom's yelling at me. Bye.

***

I haven't figured out who Pontius Pilate is but I have learned some other stuff.

I found out the church has a Mother Superior. I really want to be her and I'm pretty sure I can do it. It would be great to be called the Mother Superior. 'Mother Superior, may I help you with that?'

If I can't have kids myself I want to be the superior mother for sure. At least I won't have stretch marks like mothers get after having a baby. I'll be living in the Mother House. It will be like winning the motherlode don't you think? I know I'm being silly.

Mom says I've started to 'borrow trouble'. She says becoming a nun will 'smarten me up'. I sometimes wonder why Mom doesn't sit down and talk to me seriously about my decision to become a nun. We've started to disagree on things and this has never happened before. Our relationship is changing. That makes me sad.

***

It's a new day.

I'm learning about the Sister Superior, but not what makes her different from the Mother Superior. She might be the sister of the mother I guess.

God in Heaven, this is a complicated life I am getting myself into.

When I arrive at the convent, I'll need to find a way to change the rules about the clothes nuns wear. The long black stuff doesn't work with the image I have of myself. I haven't decided if I'll work on the fashion part before getting rid of the need to be quiet for a year, but both rules are right up there on my list of things to get changed. I'm thinking hard about all this serious stuff because I am twelve years old now and getting older every second.

I really do love going to church but sometimes it's a bit too much. We go to church every Sunday and on any occasion you can think of. Mom makes special occasions up sometimes and Dad says there is neither rhyme nor reason to her thinking. We always arrive early (really early) too.

***

I don't feel so great today.

If you must know I've started my period. How many times is this going to happen? Can you imagine walking around with blood dripping on a rag pinned inside your panties? I didn't see this coming and Mom didn't tell me a thing about it. I'm kind of pissed off to be honest.

This better not happen again – the bleeding part I mean. I couldn't stand going through this twice. I need to ask Mom a few questions.

And do you know what else pisses me off about this? I bet this doesn't ever happen to boys. E.V.E.R.

***

I know I mostly journal about my church but that's pretty much my entire life. I like getting dressed up for Sunday Mass. I have a pretty red seersucker dress I wear most Sundays with my black back-to-school patent leather shoes that really aren't back-to-school shoes at all. I pretend I get new shoes every September when school starts just like the other kids. Not true.

Speaking of school – I don't know what my brother is thinking these days but he has done something behind our parents' back and it caused a *big* fight here last night. *A rip-roaring fight.* Wilmot has quit school. He won't graduate. Everyone but him is heartbroken. Even me, because I see how much this upsets Mom and Dad. Wilmot won't tell Dad what

22

he's doing but he keeps saying he has a top-secret job for a guy named Meat (honestly that's his name.) He brags a lot and says he'll be making so much money he can pay rent to live here and buy stuff for all of us. Hearing him say that made my mother cry so loud it made me cry too.

There's more. I don't know if my parents are upset about this too, but Wilmot likes girls. Not girls like my friends but girls his age. Like Beth. She laughs at his stupid jokes and waves her hands around so she can accidentally (not) touch him on the arm when she says, "Oh Wilmot, are you always this funny?"

Earlier tonight Wilmot brought a *new* girl home. They seem to really like each other. Marie is shy at first but I got her talking. She has a job working for Meat as well and my father jumped all over that. "Well maybe you can tell me what *your* job is since my son won't give me any details." Dad frightened her.

Wilmot jumped up and wanted to leave right then but Marie handled it pretty well. "I work in the office, sir. I'm Meat's personal secretary and accountant as well. I'm really good with numbers." She acted nervous but I think that was because of how gruff Dad was being.

He turned to Wilmot again to ask about his job and when he couldn't make Wilmot talk he told them both to get out. "Get the Hell out of my house." I couldn't believe it. Then he told me to go to bed, like I'd done something wrong. I'm going to stay awake until Wilmot comes home. *If* he comes home.

How can you kick your own kid out of the house? I better remember that in the future.

***

It's official; my brother is *not* going back to school. He made the announcement just before he left after supper yesterday. Mom invited him behind Dad's back but it worked out okay. Dad says he's going to find out how Wilmot is earning so much money if it's the last thing he ever does. Dad doesn't like the way Wilmot talks about Meat either. He seems to idolize this character and Dad thinks to earn so much money and not be willing to explain how – well, Dad kind of stops at that part of the sentence. I need to talk to my brother *again*. He used to tell me everything but now I have no idea what's going on. That's not fair. Marie seems to have taken my place. Is that even possible – would a guy really let his girlfriend replace his sister? I'm not sure I want to know the answer to that question.

***

I often hear my parents whispering in their bedroom. It sounds to me like they're fighting but when I ask about it or if they're mad at me I always hear the same thing. "Oh no, Paradise, everything is okay." I don't think that's true.

My father and I have a big secret. A secret we kept from Mom for almost a year because we knew when we told her she would be totally mad at both of us. Dad's teaching me how to shoot a gun. Honest to God. He has a collection of shotguns and hunting rifles and so many other guns it makes me dizzy trying to name them all.

We go to the rifle range every Friday night. It would be better if we went on Sunday after mass because we would have more time, but can you imagine what Mom would say about us shooting on God's day? Dad says I'm a natural with a gun.

Mom says what we're doing is a sin against God and the fact that Dad has to sneak me in to the rifle range proves it. I don't care who's right and who's wrong. I just like to shoot.

If my career as a nun doesn't work out Dad says I can be a policeman. He laughs but then he always says, "Paradise, I'm not kidding. You would make a great policeman, or even a private investigator. I like the sound of that. My daughter the PI."

One day, I think I was about ten, I was in the lobby talking with our concierge when the police arrived. I was fascinated. They wore uniforms, had guns and dead serious expressions on their face. Three of them marched in – all men of course – but it made me wonder if *I* could do their job. They demanded the keys to one of the units and our concierge snapped to attention and did exactly what he was told. They had such power.

***

For once, I'm not going to journal about God or the church or my life as a nun.

Today, it's about Elvis Presley. Mom says he's too old for me. He was a sergeant in the army before I even started school. I don't care. I love his music. He had to have short hair when he was in the army but as soon as he got out he grew it long again. I *love* long hair. *Especially on Elvis.*

I also like Chubby Checker. He's doing this new dance called 'The Twist'. It's a very cool dance – I find it hard to learn how to make my body twist but I'm working on it. I'm hoping nuns can dance in private. Well, private except for God watching. I'd like to watch dance shows or *The Flintstones* more often but because Mom is hooked on the news that's mostly what we watch. Last night I got into trouble for singing this new song by Motown called 'Shop Around'. The beat's great to dance to but Mom made me sit still because the news was coming on in a few minutes and she had already told me twice to stop singing. 'Don't make me tell you twice,' is usually my final warning that trouble is heading my way.

I think Dad has been getting in trouble lately too. There's more and more quiet talk coming from my parents' bedroom. I even hear shouting. They don't seem to worry about us hearing what they say anymore. It makes me cry. Wilmot says I can talk to him about it whenever I'm upset. He's a good big brother that way but he's mostly with Marie all the time.

***

I haven't really got time to write today but I need to remember something. This is the best ever. I made Mom laugh out loud while I was singing, 'Only the Lonely'. *Then* when I sang, 'Save the Last Dance for Me' she got up and danced with me. For real. My mother can dance. By the time I get to be the Mother Superior I'll be a great dancer thanks to Mom. And, 'Save the Last Dance for Me' will be my favourite song for my whole life.

Honest to God, doing all that dancing with my mother was the best. I felt so happy inside myself.

***

Life is a mess in my house.

Something really bad happened. Dad lost his job. I didn't know it was possible for fathers to lose their job. I remember once Dad and my mom had a fight about Dad working and Mom staying at home. Dad was yelling so loud. "If you go to work people will think I can't support my family. Don't you even *think* about it."

I don't know what Dad's job was exactly. He likes to say, "I can do a hodgepodge of things, honey." I thought hodgepodge was what we have for dinner the night before payday when Mom takes everything she has left in the kitchen and makes supper out of it. (It's really good.)

Dad doesn't know this yet but Mom's already working. She gets paid $4.00 an hour doing the house cleaning for our neighbours in the apartment right across the hall. She does some sewing for them too. Mom's a great sewer.

While Dad was working, I know he got paid and stuff but when Mom told me (We were whispering while she was hemming my new skirt.) she knows she'll be able to find a better job, I started thinking a little bit differently about my future. I'll be thirteen very soon so it can't be too early to plan. Things like maybe when I get through school and grow up I'd like to earn my own money, have my own place and buy nice things.

I can't have my own place when I'm a nun, but at least I won't have to listen to a man like the one my dad has become. I'll be so glad to go to the convent right after I finish high school. I'll be eighteen by then so I better get my mind straight about whether I want to be a nun or get a job and make money. I can't do both. At least I don't think I can.

I may still be a kid but I know this for sure – I don't ever in my whole life want to have to stick my hand out and ask a man for money. I'm as good as any man already. Mom would call that 'attitude'.

I won't be able to take a gun with me when I go to the convent. I want to ask our priest if it's a sin to shoot a gun like my mother says but I am afraid of what the answer might be. I'm pretty sure I know already.

2
1969

Today's my thirteenth birthday. It's official – I'm a teenager. I want this to be a year to remember. I'm actually trying to write a song about becoming a teenager but that's not going too well. It's my first song so I know it'll be tough. I've got a few ideas though.

I haven't written here much lately. Mom says I've been busy preparing to become a teenager. She says I never finish anything I start but I don't think that's true. I hope it's not true. It's not fair either. To be honest, some days I don't think my mother knows as much as I thought she did while I was growing up.

I share more here than I do when I go to the confessional at my church and tell every little thing to our priest. "Bless me, Father, for I have sinned. These are my sins. This week I swore at my brother, I talked back to my dad, I spoke to Thomas (Yes, it's apparently a sin to even *talk* to him.), I spent too much time looking at myself in the mirror, I danced too much when I should have been sitting still, blah... blah... blah." Sometimes I think Father-know-it-all knows too much. About me I mean.

I'm having confusing thoughts about living my life as a nun. And, it's not just grown-ups like my dad that confuse me. Thomas, living right next door, with his

Elvis face and that smile – he's on my mind all the time. I see him at the shooting range almost every time Dad and I are there but I'm too shy to say more than a few words. Stupid me. He smiled at me today. And, it gets better. He said, "Happy Birthday, kid. I hear you're a teenager now. Lookin' good." Honest to God, that's what he said. I couldn't even open my mouth to say a word. I felt lost – deep in my stomach. Paradise lost.

I went straight to confession and when I told my priest, in confidence obviously, about talking to Thomas and not being sure I want to be a nun, guess what he said. In his confessional-soft voice no less, and with his trademark twenty-second delay (I time it on my watch and it's always precisely twenty seconds – a very long time when you're waiting for your penance) before he opens his mouth. "What do your parents think of your possible change of plans, Paradise?"

Are you freaking kidding me? Isn't it supposed to be a secret when you pull that confessional curtain and spill your guts? I decided to pause before answering too. I let silence be my answer. My priest knows exactly who I am and that pisses me off. It confuses me like everything else. It's not like I confessed that I let someone touch my don't-you-ever-let-anyone-touch-it. First time ever that I stood up and walked out of the confessional without saying a word in reply to a question asked by the almighty priest.

Happy Birthday to me. Colour me confused.

***

I've let more than a year go by without writing in my diary. I've been thinking about lots of things but just haven't felt like putting anything down on paper. I especially don't write all of my secrets down. One secret I'm keeping even from my diary. It's not bad or anything. It's *my* secret. For now.

There are so many things I want to do with my life. I'm fifteen and I like to set goals. So far I have quite a few goals and I write them down on a list that I keep in my pocket.

1. I want to be the greatest athlete my high school has ever seen. I'm good at every sport already. My favourites are basketball, volleyball, track and field and hockey. I have about three years left to be an even better athlete than I am today. I want to go from good to great. I will.

2. I want to grow up to be a real Aries woman. Mom and I are both Aries women and we read our horoscope together every morning. Mom gets embarrassed when it says something like, 'There will be romance this evening.' Often Mom turns to me and says, "Don't you be getting any ideas, young lady." Or, she finds a way to remind me that in a few years I'll be a nun and will belong to God.

3. When I was young I tried to win marbles from every kid I knew. I was a bit of an expert at flicking marbles to see who could get the most marbles into the hole we dug in the dirt. I bet I could still win all the marbles from the girls and most of the boys too. Now I think more about turning some of these kids into my friends. Once I heard Dad tell a friend that to get ahead at

the office they would have to 'play for all the marbles.' When I asked him about that later he said it had nothing to do with marbles. *What?* Bottom line – I would like to have more friends.

4. I want to wear one of those sexy red push-em-up-and-squeeze-em together bras. (Guess who's going to buy me one for my sixteenth birthday?) I'm not sure about taking it with me when I go to the convent though.

5. I want to be a cheerleader at our school. I kind of know I'm not pretty enough so I have almost given up on the idea. Maybe I'll grow pretty this year.

6. I want to shoot as many different types of guns as possible and be as good at shooting a gun as I was at winning marbles. I want to know everything there is to know about guns. Not very nun-like.

7. I want to write a book about my life when I'm old enough to have a life. I've learned a lot so far and keeping a diary should help me remember it all later.

8. Doing things to help other people is important to me. I don't mean like when Wilmot and I help our neighbour bring her groceries from her car to her apartment. I want to do something bigger when I'm bigger myself.

When I review my goals it doesn't sound like I'll be ready to go to the convent after I graduate from high school in a few years. I figure #8 is my greatest calling and I don't know how to do something big to help others unless it's as a nun. Clearly, I've made my decision. I have to keep telling myself that. I have to work hard to be emotionally ready when the time comes.

I'll be able to devote my entire life to helping others without the worry of getting a job, making money, having a home of my own or even worrying about how often I need to get my hair cut.

What I need to do is sit down with my mom and talk about all of this. She doesn't read my diary and she might not know about all of my goals but she definitely knows I want to become a nun. When I bring it up she mostly just smiles. "You're a good girl, Paradise." *Sure.*

And then, there's Thomas. I know he has *not* taken me seriously at all whenever I've spoken with him and shared my desire to be a nun. He has said to me so many times, "Paradise, your devotion to your church is one thing but you *do not* have to run away from me and give your life to Him."

How will I ever say goodbye?

3

1972

Bless me, Father, for I have sinned. Over and over I whisper the words. Only to myself because I dare not tell even my priest. He would tell my parents and that can't happen. It would break their hearts. Such big secrets prior to my sixteenth birthday. I feel old – this is probably what twenty feels like.

It turns out Mom has been keeping a secret too – for sixteen years. A few days ago she wanted to treat me to dinner in a restaurant. That doesn't happen in our family. 'There's plenty of food in the kitchen so no need to spend hard earned money eating out.' I've heard both of my parents utter those words on more than a few occasions when either Wilmot or I ask if we could go out for a meal. *Please.* So when Mom suggested she and I dine out I was nervous thinking of what she might know – or not know. I certainly was not prepared to learn *her* secret.

It seems my parents are *not* my parents. I was stunned to hear my mother speak the words. I was adopted from an Acadian village, Cape St Mary, in Clare, Nova Scotia when I was three years old.

"Is Wilmot adopted too?"

"No," came the short reply.

Mom felt I should have this bit of information prior to turning sixteen and if I wanted to find my birth parents she would help me after I finish school in a couple of years. In retrospect I should have asked for more detail but I was focused on something more important at the time.

For my sixteenth birthday Tomas promised he'd come home to see me. It would have to be a short visit because he's not supposed to leave basic training. Thomas is in Regina, Saskatchewan at the Royal Canadian Mounted Police (RCMP) training academy. We've been exchanging letters every week. My parents, especially Dad, feel I am too young to have a boyfriend. They don't understand. They don't *know* either.

***

I turned sixteen today. Sweet sixteen. Not so sweet for me.

Thomas came home.

We met at our secret place last night.

Thomas brought me the sexy red birthday gift he had promised. I tried it on. I loved it. He loved it too and he loved me. We danced and we made love. Everything was so beautiful. I didn't want it to end but... we had to talk.

Thomas listened without understanding. So much anger. Such harsh words spoken. He turned and walked away from me shouting, "Seriously? You choose Him over me?" I didn't have the chance to say anything else.

What began as the most beautiful day of my life ended as the absolute worst.

***

Right or wrong I have made the decision to enter the convent now rather than in two more years. I begged my parents to take me but they would have none of it. Assuming they had talked me out of what they called *an insane decision* they left me alone.

I knew it was a sin to take advantage of my brother, but I also knew he would do anything for me. I spoke to Marie first to make sure she was on my side and together we talked Wilmot in to driving me to the convent in his brilliantly yellow new car. I still didn't know what kind of work he was doing for his boss, Meat, but had stopped asking questions. Wilmot would only say, 'It's paying for my future, Paradise, and possibly yours too so don't ask.' I didn't.

This would prove to be a huge mistake on my part. Perhaps Wilmot would have given me details if I'd insisted. Even though we fought as all siblings do we would do anything for each other. Especially if one of us was in trouble.

As it turned out, I was in a heap of trouble.

While I was certain I'd made the right decision – the only decision for me – as I lay in my bed the night before leaving the only home I had ever known, I prayed that in the clear light of day, I would go to school with only the worries all sixteen-year-old girls face. I should have recognized this as doubt. I did not.

Before dawn the very next day we drove in the silence of a cold April morning – Wilmot, Marie and I. I needed the quiet time and I suspect they didn't know what to say. Wilmot hugged me as he helped me with my one small suitcase. "Call me anytime night or day, little sister, and I will be here to collect you. Promise you'll call if you need me – for anything. *I need you to say it Paradise*. Promise me."

"I promise."

I gave Wilmot a letter I had written to my parents begging their forgiveness for sneaking off this way. I knew their hearts would break as they read my words. My sixteen-year-old mind was telling me I belonged with and to God. I promised to keep in touch, if that was allowed, as I began my life as a nun. My letter did not include anything about my biggest secret of all.

Hello, God, where are you?

Part Two

An Unlikely Journey

4
1972

You don't know how little you've learned in your first sixteen years until you leave that world behind. Entering the convent years before I was emotionally or mentally prepared brought with it total shock.

The day Wilmot and Marie dropped me off I'm unsure how long I stared at nothing in particular after their car was out of sight. Eventually one of the nuns came to my rescue and helped me inside. She was kind. She had seen it many times. I wasn't even troubled by her head-to-toe black habit. In only twenty-four hours changing the wardrobe for nuns was no longer even on my list of concerns.

Now what? I found my mind moving between two worlds – in a daze both inside and my former life outside of the convent.

I had to live with my outside world turned inward. My sixteen years tucked away not to be remembered in any way as I moved forward with a total dedication to Him.

I believe most people imagine girls go into the convent because of an unsuccessful love affair. Possibly some do, but they are a rare exception.

In my world most girls become nuns because they belong to one of two classes. *The first* consists of those who are naturally devout. Marriage does not particularly attract them. They love a quiet well-ordered existence with heaven as its goal. *The second* and larger class consists of those who enter convents less because they themselves choose to do so than because they are chosen by God. These are real vocations. A spiritual adventure has happened to them – a vital encounter between their souls and God. They therefore become possessed by a burning hunger for God, which only He Himself can satisfy. They are ready to trample underfoot the world and everything in it. All communication with the outside world is reduced to the absolute minimum. Newspapers and secular literature are prohibited, visits and letters suppressed or censored. In part, one lives, as much as humanly possible, oblivious of what goes on outside the convent walls. Truthfully I did miss hearing the news. I get that from my mother. She could *never* miss the news.

I don't think I belonged to, or was comfortable with, either of the two classes. Not sure what that says about me.

Almost the first thing the Mistress of Novices explained to me was the importance of being exact about even the smallest details. "You must give up your own tastes and allow yourself to be moulded according to the pattern of the Order to which you now belong." Huh?

In that moment my mind was a million miles away. I tried to picture my parents reading the letter I had left for them. And, that was the easy part. I couldn't get Thomas out of my mind. Both of my parents had tried to drill into me that 'Looks are not important'. The long blonde hair. The oh-so-square chin. The soft yet gruff voice that made me feel good about myself. Not important? I definitely needed to bury those memories.

Silently I was singing 'Save the Last Dance for Me'.

Life in the convent comes with rules, rules and more rules. Among other things, the Rules of Modesty dictated that when walking you *never* swing your arms. It seemed like a small thing to be making such a fuss over. Your hands must be clasped together at your waist. To hurry was a breach of decorum. You were obliged to walk quietly. Head bent forward and eyes modestly cast down. The idea of this guard of the senses was to help one concentrate on shutting off from the mind everything external so the faculties were kept free from memory, thought and desire of everything but God.

Adhering to the Rules of Modesty kept me so busy I didn't have time to think back to my youthful concerns – what I would wear, how quiet I must be or, God forbid, the need for a television. I was too busy to miss watching television. I was so young. So naive. So innocent. So unprepared.

Waking up in the convent was totally different from the life I had known. One does not awaken with the sound of an alarm clock or at your leisure. You awaken to the ringing of a heavy iron bell. A *loud* heavy iron bell. I was once appointed to do the early morning calling with the bell, which meant getting up half an hour earlier. After ringing the bell I went from cell to cell opening each door wide enough to hear the answers when I uttered the salutation, "Deo Gratias." (Thanks be to God.) Some of the nuns were up by the time you'd get to their cell, but many needed more than one Deo Gratias before they were ready to begin the day. I could relate.

The rooms assigned to each of us were called cells. *Honest to God.* My cell, like all of the others, was furnished with a single bed (more like a cot) a tiny dresser and a chair. Small, bare and plain – kind of like me. No one may enter your cell except the Mistress of Novices or the nurse if you should fall ill. Your cell is a place of silence – doors and windows must be opened noiselessly. No sound must break the stillness – neither the sound of a voice nor passing feet. I even tried to *breathe* quietly when I was alone. God forbid I should breathe too loudly or dare to speak in the confines of my cell. *Bless me, Father, that sounds sarcastic and I know better.* (None of this is easy and as I move forward I'm surprised to learn none of it comes naturally. Not fun and no comfort either.)

When I entered the convent it was mandatory to bring a dowry, to be returned if you should make the decision to leave. Wilmot donated my dowry of $100.00 at the last minute. You were not allowed to have money in your possession overnight – not even a penny that you may have picked up on a walk. If you found a penny and failed to give it to the Mistress until the following day, you must seek forgiveness by asking for a penance against your vow of obedience. Your penance might be begging for your dinner. I never got used to that. You would have to approach the most senior nuns. Perhaps one nun would give you a slice of toast. The next nun would take it away from you and you might be left with just salt and pepper and even then you would have to ask permission of the Mistress to eat your dinner.

I will be honest and admit that I swore under my breath the first time I had to beg for my dinner consisting of pepper. Seriously, nothing but pepper on my plate. Good God Almighty.

One memorable for all the wrong-reasons day I was assigned kitchen duty. Around four p.m. one of the junior postulants asked what time she should put the eggs in the steamer. To this day I swear I said at twenty minutes to six. She thought I said in twenty minutes. I walked by the steamer at about a quarter to five and saw the yolks bouncing out toward the drain. Because I was in charge of the kitchen I naturally had to take the blame. As I put the eggs into a pail to show the Mistress I was horrified to see such a waste of twelve dozen eggs. You can only imagine my penance, to say nothing about my infractions against my vows of poverty and obedience.

I thought I would be happier. I thought I would be more content. I *didn't* think I would miss Thomas so much – my Thomas. *Dear God in Heaven I pray I have not made a mistake?* I want, no I need, my total focus to be on Him. Why can't I do that?

5

1973

Life with Wilmot was wonderful but working for Meat was more than Marie could cope with. It was affecting their lives.

Marie typed all of Meat's letters and kept his spreadsheets current and accurate. "What exactly am I tracking here, Meat? What's bringing in so much money? *So much cash*?" Marie needed to know. She didn't trust her boss.

More than once Meat had slapped Marie and followed up with the threat to *beat her silly* if she didn't shut up and, "Just keep typing like I pay you to do." He always made it sound as if she had done something wrong. She knew she was better than this. She deserved better and so did Wilmot.

Marie knew she had to talk to Wilmot after one violent slap from Meat that had thrown her to the ground. She worried Wilmot would go straight to Meat and was unsure who would come out the victor if the two took to fighting. Wilmot was a scrapper but Meat was a trained fighter. Still, they had to do something. They had to get away.

On the night they spoke about all of this they promised to be totally honest with each other. Marie spoke first. She shared her concerns about not understanding what Wilmot's job consisted of as well as the ugly fact Meat had been slapping her. In fact, he was beating her. If she was going to continue to track dollars she wanted to know what was behind all the money they were bringing in. She wanted to be respected and wasn't sure Meat understood the word *respect*. It appeared Wilmot was doing the dirty work while Meat stayed out of sight waiting for the money come in.

Wilmot slowly and carefully outlined his job as he held Marie in his arms. He made it sound legitimate. He hoped it was. As she listened, Marie's heart was breaking. She was certain Wilmot too had been beaten into submission. She should have known. If Meat was slapping her he was doing much worse to Wilmot.

Wilmot had risen to be Meat's *main man*. He almost said it with pride. This was why; he explained without looking at Marie, he was making so much money. All the money they were saving was due to how successful the business was with him leading the way. Marie reminded Wilmot she still didn't know what he did every day. Details please. Wilmot had no choice but to share the ugly truth about his job.

Meat was working with many different organizations but mainly the Catholic Children's Aid Society. For example, and Wilmot paused before he went on, he began many of his mornings driving to a convent to pick up a newborn. Meat told him specifically where to go and he went. "You don't have to think Wilmot, just do what you're told," would be Meat's response whenever Wilmot dared to ask questions.

Marie couldn't believe what she was hearing. She had suspected drugs… but this? Why would a mother sell her baby? When she asked the question Wilmot paused once again.

"I don't know the details because Meat handles all of that. I just show up to get the baby and take it wherever I'm told. I *am* a bit worried about it to tell you the truth, Marie. I just hope the moms know what they're doing when they sell their baby. I guess they give some of the money to the convent where they stayed until they have the kid but… please, I don't know the details, Marie, so stop asking. We buy the baby and then sell it for a huge profit. I know it doesn't sound right. We get way more money than the baby's mother receives and that's a fact. Don't judge me, Marie, I'm following orders." Wilmot hung his head.

They talked until well into the night and both were drained when they finally went to bed. The hard decisions had been made. Wilmot would go to Meat in the morning and quit his job. He would make it clear Marie was done with the business as well. Together they would move away leaving Meat and all of his activities behind. They were foolish to assume it would be that simple.

The nasty underbelly of profit in baby selling would foil all of their plans.

Wilmot returned to their flat late the following evening barely able to walk or see having been beaten almost beyond recognition. Meat had not taken the news well and Wilmot left with the clear understanding he was still on the payroll. Meat, and no one else, would dictate his fate. At least Meat accepted the fact Marie was done working for him.

The news of Marie's departure didn't seem to bother Meat at all. Wilmot should have paid more attention to that part of their discussion.

He found his beautiful Marie covered in blood lying just inside the door. Wilmot couldn't find a pulse and was sure she was dead. He called for help while saying a silent prayer to Paradise's God. *Help her please. Let her live.* Wilmot knew when the police saw the battered state of both of them there would be questions. Too many questions. He had no choice but to run.

Wilmot cradled Marie in his arms until he heard the ambulance approach. Kissing her one last time he gently touched her battered face before he slipped out the side door. He whispered a second prayer asking God to let her live. With the pain and stress of everything falling down around him Wilmot knew he had one last thing to do before Meat caught up with him.

Paradise would never forgive Wilmot for breaking his promise to her. Yet, he knew he had to make one phone call before he disappeared. Until this moment, Wilmot had done everything his sister asked of him and he had kept her secret. He couldn't any longer. With nervous energy and another prayer Wilmot placed a long distance call to Thomas. It was not lost on Wilmot that he had done a lot of praying in the last twenty-four hours. That would be the influence of his sister.

6

1977

The unkindness towards me in my time of grief when I first learned Wilmot was missing played a significant role in my decision to walk away from a life devoted to God. *My brother was missing.*

I was not told how Mother Superior received the news – merely summoned to her quarters, told to sit and pray in silence until she was able to join me. When Mother Superior arrived, her words broke my heart. "Your brother is missing and apparently has been for a while. His woman friend, Marie, seems to be gone too. Now go back to your chores. Prayers will be necessary so you can forgive those who may have done them harm." Sweet Mother of God, where was God's hand in this? I begged to be allowed to return home to be with my parents at this time. Request denied.

Life in the convent began to wear me down – wear down the depths of my commitment. With all the unhappiness I was feeling every day I longed for only one thing. I wanted to go home.

The day came when I could no longer hide from the truth. I was *not* suited to be a nun. Truthfully, I never was. With my mind made up I talked to the Mistress about my wishes. There were moments when I told myself if I left the convent I would go to hell. There were moments when I told myself I was living in hell. I had to leave. I had failed although I wondered if perhaps the failure would be in staying.

Our Father who art in Heaven forgive me my damn sins.

***

Leaving the convent behind was as uneventful as the return to my childhood home. My parents arrived at the appointed time and we drove home in silence – five years had passed – we had nothing to say. No questions, no comments – on either side. Everything between us seemed formal and stiff, yet I felt confident we could work together to make things better over time. In fairness to Mom and Dad we had not spoken with each other since the last night I lived under their roof – my sixteenth birthday. When we went to bed that night, Mom and Dad had no idea I would be gone when they awoke the next morning.

There was so much my parents didn't know. The car was filled with strangers. Three of us. All strangers.

After the secrecy of the convent, and all that happened while I was there, trying to fit in to the real world, as so many call it, has been, in some ways, harder than leaving home. When I wake up nothing seems real. I had not been more than a few hours out of the convent when I realized I didn't know anything about modern life. At the very least, it felt that way.

The world has moved forward but I have not. During my initial attempts to adjust to the outside world, the most difficult thing to deal with was my own attitude. In part, my attitude had not matured while I lived in my cell.

Even money was an issue. I didn't know the cost of anything. I wasn't comfortable calling money my own and was forever counting my change just for practice. My lack of confidence was huge.

As I finalized my plans to leave the convent I became increasingly worried about my brother. I tried numerous times without success to reach Wilmot and then Marie. I simply *could not* find them. Maybe Wilmot needed me. He was there for me in my time of need and I wanted to return the favour.

I will always cherish the memory of entering my bedroom in my parents' home and the feeling of comfort that washed over me. My room was exactly as I had left it. The journal I began on my sixteenth birthday was sitting on my small desk waiting for me. My goodness, it had been a very long time since I sat down with my trusted journal. In the convent all journal entries were in my head. We were not permitted to keep a personal diary. There were so many things we were not permitted to do.

I left my cell with such mixed feelings but one thing is certain. My love for Him will never diminish. I will move forward with Him always in my heart and I know he will guide me.

My father gave me a gift just hours after we arrived home. He gave me a gun! And it's a beauty. A nine-millimetre Beretta. He also gave me the shoulder strap and holder to go with it. The softest leather you can imagine. Says it will come in handy when I become a private investigator. I wonder.

***

It startles me to realize I have been home for just over a year and have not yet made any major decisions about my life. It's definitely time to make a few but for some strange reason I'm not there yet. I still feel a bit stuck. In limbo.

My music is playing as I write. How I missed my music.

During my first two years in the convent we had one hour of free time in the morning and another in the afternoon. This was when we made friends and created memories. We sang. We danced. Oh, how we danced. The music was old and our dance moves were not all that current, but we laughed and we cried and we did it together. We pledged our lifelong friendship to each other.

How I longed to hear my own music while in my cell. I wanted to sing out loud 'I've Got You Babe' by Sonny and Cher, and 'Walk Don't Run' by the Ventures, which could be my theme song now, I guess.

No, my theme song has to be Gloria Gaynor's new song 'I Will Survive'. I vow to not only survive but to thrive.

I am now able to relive memories I was forbidden to recall in the convent. So many seemingly small things are gifts at this very moment. I remember so clearly the Sunday night in February 1964 when the Beatles were on the *Ed Sullivan Show*. At the time I thought I would die with excitement. I sang and danced through every second of their performance. I was eight years old.

From my cell I often wondered what songs were on the hit parade compared to my last day at home when my mother and I danced one last time to 'You've Lost That Lovin' Feeling'.

Did she realize why I was crying?

To this day, I have not lost that 'lovin' feeling' for Thomas. I want to know everything about him. What has he been doing these six long years? I assume he is still with the RCMP. I do know he doesn't live in Toronto. My father found a way to let that information drop as soon as we arrived home. "Your partner in crime left town with his tail between his legs, so don't bother thinking he will be sniffing around here."

I'll ask about Thomas when I get the nerve. Today is not that day.

***

I know I can't live at home with my parents forever, or even for much longer. I'm not sure downtown Toronto is my true place in the world either. I once did but not anymore. I have roots in another part of the country and I have to square my shoulders and tackle that. I will – soon.

I have met with the police and they confirmed Wilmot is truly missing. They're calling it a cold case with no one assigned to it at the moment. I desperately need to find him and make sure he's okay. Wilmot's absence in our lives has left an empty space in our hearts and in our parents' home. I want to find Marie too. I suspect she could use a friend and I know I could. The Toronto police force advised me Marie is missing as well and they suspect she may have been murdered. Hearing those words shocked me. I could not and would not believe Marie is dead.

I feel confident enough to admit, finally, that I *really do* want to become a private investigator. I have the literature to begin the process of applying for the courses required to achieve my goal.

First though, it's about me and the first few years of my life.

My name is Paradise d Rhodes. I need to understand the circumstances surrounding my adoption. What does the lower case d in my name stand for? What was my birth name? Who holds the answers I need?

7
1979

My d in lower case has significant meaning after all. It's not my middle initial as I had always assumed but part of my last name. *That thought had not entered my mind.* My birth name is Paradise d'Entremont.

Everything about my life is different at the moment and my learning curve is huge. I have returned to an Acadian village in rural Nova Scotia. I was born in this area albeit I have no memory of my life here. My address is RR #3, Meteghan River, Nova Scotia. When I was three years old I was adopted and moved from Meteghan River to downtown Toronto in the arms of the couple I would call my mother and father.

While in the convent I was able to complete my high school credits and several university level courses. I'm now making plans to build on that. There are PI courses I can investigate not far from where I live. Things are happening quickly. I may have been idle for too long when I first left the convent but I am making up for lost time now. I'm learning about life, about how to live on a daily basis and about my past. Everything I learn makes me eager to know more.

I have my first apartment. It may not look like much to others but it's a mansion to me. In total it's not much bigger than my bedroom back in Toronto – I have a small living space plus a bathroom and a tiny kitchen. It all adds up to my very own private piece of the world. Total privacy and alone-time whenever I want it is a huge gift I have given myself. In reality I could have found a larger apartment if I wanted a roommate to help with the rent but I'm allowing myself to make this *all about me.*

I've learned to pay my bills on time and am happy to have as many jobs as I can get. Keeping busy waiting tables and washing dishes at the local coffee shop is a great way to meet people. I clean houses for several people including those who feel such work is beneath them. I don't mind doing their dirty work at all. They pay me well. My third job is very interesting and another great way to meet the locals. I sort through bins and bins of clothing at the local second-hand store, Frenchy's. Everyone, and I do mean everyone, knows about Frenchy's. People drive from all over to shop there. Bargains for everyone.

I don't mind working all day every day. That will change but I'm okay with it for now.

It's hard to explain how I felt when I began thinking about finding my birth mother. I thought I would die if I didn't find her and I thought I would die if I did. Similar to those life and death feelings I had about leaving, or not leaving, the convent. I do feel closer to my birth mother now that I'm living here.

Meteghan is a small community. When I began to look for answers, I made the mistake of asking anyone I spoke with about the history of the community and residents dating back to the mid-fifties. Everyone had a different story. None seemed all that accurate and some were less than believable. Then I found a wonderful research library at the local university near by. The library became my refuge.

In the back of my mind I knew I could ask Monsignor Sidney to help me. He had been in the Meteghan area for his entire life. Both before and after he was the Monsignor he knew what was going on. However, I was still angry with God because I had asked for help once and help was not there. I felt I had been-there-done-that and was not going there again. As a 'retired nun' I am working hard to resolve my issues with the church. My anger with Him is hurting no one but me.

One of my best friends in the convent, Sister Mary Elizabeth, shared a quote with me and I have made it my personal mantra. 'Fool me once shame on you. Fool me twice shame on me.' This makes sense to me and I think it can be applied to almost everything I do. For sure there are those who would fool me more than once if I let it happen. I am a bit too trusting in some instances but learning as I go. It's not a comfortable feeling for me, *not yet anyway*, to constantly have my guard up around others. I often wonder how much I actually missed while I was in the convent. Part of it was my youth when I left home. At sixteen I really hadn't formed my own identity. I'm working hard to create that now. 'Sense of self' is what one of my customers, Adeline, at the coffee shop calls it. Adeline says I'm searching for myself. We have great chats when she comes in for coffee and I have time to sit with her. She is quite elderly but has lived a very full life and I love listening to her stories.

I miss Sister Mary Elizabeth. We had a connection – not only spiritual but in life skills. We shared *so many* secrets concerning events at the convent. I find I'm not ready to address the heart breaking details of some of the goings-on. At least not yet. We didn't understand and we were unable to confirm anything at the time. It wasn't lost on any of the young pregnant women that *things were going on.* They were all simply too focused on their own pregnancy and the whole birthing process they faced at such a young age. I don't think any of us had even a fleeting thought of *taking on the establishment.*

For all my research and scientific fact-checking, the most accurate information about my birth parents and the first three years of my life would be shared as I sat on the dock on Cape St Mary Road in Mavillette watching the fishing boats come and go during high and low tides.

I lived for thirteen years in the center of downtown Toronto among the high-rise buildings and concrete jungle and called it home. From the time I was three years old until I left I assumed everyone lived as we did. We could walk around the block and within an hour be at the bank, post office, grocery store, dry cleaners, the drug store and back home before the coffee pot was cold. Where I live now, not so much.

Yet, at this moment I'm so much more at home sitting on this dock listening to the sound of silence than ever before. *This* feels like home.

For days – weeks – I knew the old and weathered fisherman was watching me out of the corner of his eye. He had a stare that said so much. 'I know what you need to know. I know who you are. I know who your mama is.' Finally, at day's end, and a fisherman's day is always a long one, he approached me. He sat on the stoop in my direct view. It was truly the sunniest of days. "What brings you here, little one? I've seen you around these parts quite a bit lately."

"Looking for my mother. And, my dad too. I need to know who my birth parents are and why they gave me away. I was born here so I'm hoping I can find them. Can you help me, sir?"

"Sir?" His reply came with a grin that showed well-cared-for teeth, white and gleaming in the last of the day's rays. "No one has ever called me, sir. Not in these parts and not back home on the Rock either." His smile warmed my spirit and the deep tanned lines around his smiling eyes told me I could trust him. He had lived.

"I'll be after tellin' you what you want to know but I need to think about it first. Meet me back here tomorrow."

"I'll be waiting right here – same time tomorrow."

Tomorrow came and went.

Where is my fisherman who holds the key to my past?

8
1979

The old fisherman had a million thoughts running through his weary mind. Talking to himself was helping sort through it all. His mind was racing. His past wasn't finished with him yet. It was hard but he was trying to remember everything.

Was it possible? Could it actually be Paradise? The eyes, the smile and the tilt of her head all suggested it was indeed her. *Our little Paradise has come home. All those years gone by. Where was she at for so long?*

"Teach me, Pops. Teach me what you and Daddy are doin'." He could still hear the three-year-old stories she whispered as she sat on his lap. Paradise had a fisherwoman's eyes and ears even at that young age. Eyes and ears that saw everything, heard everything, spoke volumes and begged when begging was what she thought might work.

If he could find the nerve to tell her what she needed to know, where would he begin? *My own son was still a boy in my eyes and my grandson had only just gone seventeen when he went and got his girl pregnant.*

"Damn that boy." That's what everyone said back then. Everyone but Pops. He was closer to his grandson than to his own son. Not that he wasn't proud of his son – he did well for himself in the end. His life had never been easy. It was often that way in Newfoundland.

Pops knew Paradise was back. There were no secrets on the street.

Gossip comes cheap and folks have done their share of gossipin' about this gal since the day she came to town. She's sittin' on the dock pretty much every day. She's writin' somethin' too. And lookin'. She does lots of lookin'.

It was me who finally talked first. I started this and now I've got to keep it goin'. I don't want her leavin' anytime soon. To be honest I don't ever want this angel to leave.

I have to tell her the whole story and damn if I'm goin' to let the girl see an old fool cry. I'm after tellin' her every detail – but only when I get it all-straight in my mind. It's been hidin' somewhere in the back of my head all these years.

I'll bring Paradise some dried fish. Her mother loved it even with all the stink.

***

I didn't drop back by yesterday like I said I would. I was chicken.

I started out to meet up with Paradise but my head wouldn't let me. I needed to keep walkin' was all. I know her heart will break when I tell her the story she's after needin' to hear. Mine will break tellin' it. Today... Today's the day.

"I know I'm late, little one."

She spoke before he reached her at the end of the pier. "No problem at all. I'm glad you're here. Do you know my mother? Is she coming? Is my dad with you?"

Pops wanted to turn around and run before he reached Paradise. He knew she'd be filled with questions. Such sad eyes today. He had all the answers she needed to hear. "How much do you want to know?"

"All of it. Every detail – please don't spare me anything. I'm tough, believe me."

"I'm after bettin' you are. We'll take this in stages I think. Today, the beginning. How does that sound?"

"Perfect."

Pops moved a bit closer and sat down. "Okay, Paradise, get your Helen Reddy on. Ready to roar?"

Paradise thought her mind was playing tricks on her. He knows how much I love music. How is that even possible? *I am woman, hear me roar* is an understatement. Maybe he loves music as much as I do. And, he keeps up with current songs too.

For days Pops had been trying to think back to all those years ago. So much to remember and keep straight before spilling the words his mind was trying to organize. His story began as he held Paradise's gaze.

***

"Remember now Paradise. I have to dig some deep to go back all those years. I'm after tellin' you the story exactly as I remember it. So in my head I'm goin' back there.

"Years ago...

"Cole, my favourite and most promisin' grandson, came runnin' down the pier hand in hand with his lovely young girlfriend. These two had been together every wakin' second of every day since they first met at a softball game when they were but eleven years old.

"'Pops, we have a million things to tell you. And, we're telling you first because we loves you the most.' I remember thinkin' oh-oh, somethin' is wrong. I'm bein' buttered up for no apparent reason. Or, maybe somethin' is right. Cole had been applyin' for a whole lot of university scholarships. Madeline wanted to go to the police academy just a few miles up the line from where she lived. She could already shoot a gun like a man (I don't say that out loud too often cuz I said it once and landed in a heap of trouble.) Maybe Cole's ship had come in. No pun intended. What I was certain of – this young man would not labour at sea as I had done my entire life to only just make ends meet. This lad would have an education like no one else carryin' the d'Entremont name in these parts of Atlantic Canada. Cole d'Entremont is going to be somebody. My mind had wondered a bit as I

listened to the kids in all their excitement. They soon got my attention and continued with their story.

"'Please, Pops, just listen,' Cole continued. 'Don't get mad at us. At least not 'til you hear how we gots everything figured out. And, please don't say a word to Mom and Dad until we tell 'em. They're going to be upset and disappointed and we ain't quite ready for that.'

"Cole already had a great education but now and then he slipped into my way of talkin' even though I was tryin' to do better with my own words. I could see his excitement and hear it in his voice. Cole knew he had my full attention. Holdin' Madeline's hand even tighter he spilled it all.

They were quittin' school.

Getting' jobs.

Gettin' an apartment.

Gettin' married.

Gettin' a baby.

What? What in God's name?

"Only the baby's birth came with a specific timeline. Everythin' else was up in the air. They figured Madeline was four months pregnant so they were after bein' parents in about five months. Dear Mother of God, could this really be happenin'? I thought my heart would break but I couldn't let my emotions show. If this lad ever needed me he needed me in that moment.

"When my good wife died I packed up and left Paradise Bay, Newfoundland. I made myself a comfortable livin' here in Mavillette. I bought a big old

house at the end of Cape St Mary Road and I call it home. It was once a sea captain's house but years of neglect left it run-down and inexpensive so I was able to buy it and pay cash. I'm proud of that to be honest. My fishin' boat isn't much but it's paid for too. My life may not look like much to others but it's a clean livin'. It's comfortable and simple, just how I like it.

"When things got real tough for my son back on the Rock he asked me to take Cole and raise him as my own. There was room in my big old house and in my heart too. Cole is my treasure. I wanted everything for him. I wanted more than clean and comfortable for him. I bit my tongue as I listen to the rest of their not-so-well-thought-out plan.

"Madeline and Cole were hopin' they could bunk in with me until they save enough money for their own place. Cole asked if he could fish with me until he found whatever that job is he's after gettin'. Madeline would cook and clean while the men fish if that was okay with me.

"Cook and clean? Instead of the police academy? Gentle Jesus, these two are supposed to be the new generation. I didn't know it was a Mrs degree our Madeline was after gettin' with all that schoolin' she had already done. I had no choice but to set 'em straight. They couldn't give up their career opportunities. I took a deep breath.

"I looked first at Madeline and then at Cole – straight in the eye. 'Yes. Move in with me. Yes. Fish with

me. Yes. I'll help you make this work. But, understand one thing – both of you will be after havin' the careers you want to have right alongside of raisin' that little baby you're carryin'.' I gave them both a hug and walked away to give them a bit of privacy. I knew what they was thinkin.'

Sitting on the windowsill that day, after sharing their story, two seventeen-year-olds shared a smile that said it all. "That went well. Seriously well. Pops is right beside us all the way. Just like we knew he would be."

9
1956

They were both seventeen. Cole wore more teenaged skin than Madeline – he had some serious maturing to do. Madeline seemed, in many ways, wise beyond her years. She was focused on helping Cole grow up before the baby joined their little family. At the very least Madeline felt he had to *grow up a bit.*

Shortly after sharing their news with Pops the trio walked to the local courthouse. Each wore the very best clothes they owned. It was all *good enough.* 'I now pronounce you husband and wife.' Done.

They settled into a routine – family of three soon to be four. Pops had done so much for Cole and his wife and they were grateful. Madeline wasn't sure Cole was doing the right thing by including Pops in *everything* they did. They were never alone anymore. She would just have to make the best of it as her mother used to say – back when she had her mother. *Make the best of it girl. Just make the best of it.* Madeline could see her mother shouting the words at her when she was about six years old. Folks used to say her mother meant well but was a bit sick in the head. "I wish you were here with me now Mom,"

Madeline whispered as she washed a few clothes she had made for the baby in the early months of her pregnancy.

Madeline reached for a smoke. She almost forgot to remember – she quit smoking when they first realized they made a baby. Those Friday nights spent in their secret place just up the line in Paradise, Nova Scotia, had caught up with them. *Good God Almighty,* how would they raise a kid and still get their education? They had a real stupid fight when Cole first suggested they ask Pops if they could move in with him. Madeline guessed there was not much difference between a stupid fight and a smart fight. She hardly ever fought with Cole. She loved him too much. But, she wasn't as sure as Cole that moving in with his grandfather was the right thing to do.

As usual Pops came through. They moved in and quickly called his Cape St Mary home their home too. Madeline's dream of having her own place would have to wait. Pop's house had all the potential she hoped theirs would have. It was badly neglected though and there was no money to fix it up. The high ceilings needed work, as did the staircase. The only bathroom in the house was in rough shape. As for style – well, that was another story. Re-decorating was not discussed. Maybe after the baby came Madeline would make a few inexpensive suggestions.

For now things would stay as they were. Pops liked his Maritime theme consisting of an anchor above the bar. In this case the bar was a twenty-four of beer sitting on an overturned orange crate. Good enough.

The smell of smoke was adding to Madeline's morning sickness even though Pops and Cole had both quit smoking right along with her. Smoke had crept into everything from furniture to the few gift boxes she had brought with her. Madeline loved to Christmas shop all year long. She loved buying gifts for others.

Pops was quick to say he purchased all of his furniture at a local second-hand store and they could replace it if they wanted to. Secretly Madeline hoped they would move into their own place before they could even think of helping Pops redecorate.

Every day was the same. Madeline tried to not complain. The men rose at four thirty to head down to their fishing boat to earn a day's keep. She got up and made breakfast for her guys. She packed lunches and hearty snacks so they would be well fed all day. Madeline would eat later if she could keep anything down. Long days all around.

Madeline didn't have many girlfriends. From the day she and Cole fell in love she hadn't made time for anyone but him. She had all she needed in Cole. Too late, she realized thinking like that was a huge mistake. Her friends had moved on without her and she couldn't blame them. She was terribly lonely during the day.

Elise was the exception to Madeline's motto *no-one-but-my-Cole*. Almost daily Madeline would see Elise walking down the road toward their house. She knew she would share a few laughs with her friend. She needed to laugh. Life was much harder than she had imagined.

Elise, like Madeline, had grown up poor – dirt poor. They joked no one would ever hear them imitate the rich girls in school who loved to talk about their money. "If we're going up the line this weekend I'll need to ask Mother for a bit more money." There was no mother and there was no money. Kind of a sad thing to have in common, but it created a bond between these two young women that would exist until life's end.

Life's end would come all too soon.

It seemed Elise was enjoying this pregnancy more than Madeline. For one thing she wasn't puking every day – she tried to help in any way she could. Each visit would bring yet another find from the local Frenchy's store. If you have to pass a used-clothing store, why not drop on by and purchase something for the baby? Sometimes Elise bought a treat for Madeline too – a top or maybe a pair of pants with some sort of a stretch-belly even though it didn't look like Madeline was gaining enough weight to need a bigger pair of pants. Elise worried about her friend. She knew Madeline was not going to the doctor even though she told Cole she was. No money for a doctor. Elsie was shocked when Madeline confided in her that she had lied to Cole.

Madeline was feeling more and more tired. She figured she was in her eighth month now and it seemed she could sleep all day after her men left for the sea. The alarm clock was always set for five p.m. She wanted to be wide-awake and have supper on the stove when Pops and Cole walked through the door. She knew they liked the smell of supper. Some days it was all she could do to smile.

Madeline took pride in making sure their home was clean and well organized. Maritimers are proud of their homes regardless of what they have. The most humble of homes is one to be proud of. Lately, though, Madeline knew she was slipping with her housekeeping chores. She tried. It was all too much.

Around the time she figured her due date was closing in on her Madeline made an appointment to see the local doctor. She was concerned something might be wrong because she could hardly stay awake. No energy – day or night. She knew the doctor would be upset with her for not ensuring both she and her baby were monitored on a regular basis during her pregnancy. That was in the past. It was time to be brave and find out what the doctor had to say.

Brian, their local doctor, had married one of Madeline's classmates. Maybe that was another reason she had stayed away. Her classmate married money as they say and never let anyone forget it. She talked about money all the time and even introduced herself as 'Mrs Doctor Brian'. Did she give up her first name too *for God's sake*? She was definitely proud of her Mrs degree. Their wedding had been the talk of the town. Doctor Brian was wealthy and surely twenty years older than his bride. Madeline knew that added to the local gossip. For some girls, money trumps everything. Perhaps even love. Madeline found that profoundly sad.

Madeline and Cole had had their own perfect little wedding and the piece of paper to prove it. Baby d'Entremont would have all the love in the world.

***

Cole would not go fishing tomorrow. He was anxious to be with Madeline for her doctor's appointment. Pops would fish on his own.

The birth of the wee baby was often the number one topic of discussion while the men were fishing. Cole reminded Pops he would not fish with him tomorrow and went on to say he had been worried when Madeline woke up this morning. She confessed she was too tired to even raise her head off the pillow. She tried to reassure Cole she would be fine – he wasn't so sure. "I'll rest all day, I promise, just please don't expect supper on the table when you come home tonight," Madeline said with just a hint of a smile.

As the hours passed Cole wondered if he should have stayed home. The words were barely out of his mouth when Pops said, "We're goin' home, son. Turn this boat around and let's go and sit with Madeline. You'll have her at that fancy doctor's office before you can blink an eye." Even Pops sounded worried. "Let's hurry up though so we can be sure our girl and that baby are both okay."

"Roger that, Pops. Roger that."

10

Earlier that morning

She was still in bed. As soon as the men were out of the house Madeline had tried to sit up. There was blood everywhere.

Oh my dear Lord. She should have been honest with Cole before he left. He'd asked if she wanted him to stay with her. "No, you'll be with me tomorrow. Today you fish with Pops." If only she could take those words back. She should have said, "Stay with me Cole. I'm frightened. Help me get to the hospital. Please."

Pops had made a fire in the stove before the men left, but the breeze was cooler than it should be at this time of the year and Madeline was cold – so cold. Why hadn't she listened to Pops when he wanted to have the phone line repaired after a recent storm? Trying to prove how tough she was Madeline had insisted their money could be better spent. "No phone needed here." Wrong.

Even though Elise had not planned to visit today, Madeline prayed that she would surprise her and drop on by.

Madeline slowly got out of bed. Or tried. She fell to the floor with the first pain. This must be what childbirth is like. *Jesus, Mary and Joseph.* Who knew it would be this bad?

The fire had gone out – *freezing*. What time is it – *lost track*. Baby coming – *now*.

She had literally no time to think. Madeline reached between her legs and cradled her baby's head. *Her baby's head.*

Time stood still and yet it seemed a million years passed. There was so much pain. Lifting her newborn to her belly Madeline felt a love she had never experienced. A girl. Their baby girl. Cole would be so proud of her and would fall instantly in love with his daughter. She did it. All by herself. And, she had saved so much money in doctor's and hospital bills. Madeline had never been happier.

All too soon she realized something was terribly wrong. She was bleeding profusely. *So much blood.* Madeline had no way to stop the red river flowing from her tired young body. She could do nothing to help herself.

"Need to keep my baby warm until Cole gets here. Are you warm, baby girl?" Madeline was in near panic as she wrapped her daughter in every blanket she could reach.

Crawling to the kitchen table, Madeline reached up to grab a piece of paper and a pencil. With tears blinding her vision, she gently placed a note on her daughter's chest. A note consisting of four words.

Four words that would be her last.

11

Later the same day

Cole and Pops docked their fishing boat and, still dressed for the sea, ran up Cape St Mary Road to home and Madeline.

Not a word was spoken but they were thinking the same thing. Something is wrong. Very wrong. No spiral of smoke rising from the chimney. No lights. No sign of Madeline at the window to welcome her men home from the sea.

Please let Madeline and the baby be okay.

Cole pushed through the door with Pops not far behind. They saw it at the same time. The faint red stain on the worn braided rug in the living room. From the bedroom Cole and Pops heard the faintest of cries. "Pops, it's Madeline. I hear her. She must be resting in bed." *Thank you, God.* Pops wasn't so sure it was Madeline they heard crying. It wasn't his place to enter their bedroom first as they followed the trail of blood so without breaking his long stride Pops guided Cole ahead of him.

Indeed, the whimpering had not come from Cole's beloved wife. The red stain became brighter as it trailed from the rug to the oilcloth in the bedroom. There on the floor lay what appeared to be the smallest of babies wrapped in multiple blankets – whimpering so quietly they could barely hear the cries.

Lying on her side, holding her daughter's tiny hand Madeline was clad only in her bloodstained nightgown. Blood everywhere. Her face appeared so peaceful one could almost hope she was sleeping. Pops and Cole knew this was not the case. *Her body was cold to the touch.*

How could this be possible? How could they lose Madeline? Dear God in Heaven. Bless her soul. Pops died a thousand deaths as he watched his boy. He knew they were in a real live nightmare. One they would never forget.

Cole threw himself on top of Madeline in an attempt to warm her body. He tried to bring her back to life. He needed her. *Their baby needed her.*

Pops knew it was not to be. Madeline was dead. She died in childbirth.

Cole would be the first to read the crumpled note pinned to the top blanket covering the tiny child. Pops tried his best not to hover as he watched his grandson come to grips with the scene. He waited for a few more seconds then tried to nudge Cole into fatherhood in a hurry. They had a baby to tend to. She seemed to have a good set of lungs and she was not about to stop crying.

The baby cried a bit louder as if to say, "I'm here. Someone help me for God's sake." Cole looked from Madeline to the baby. His baby. He read the note, seeming to see the words but not understanding what they meant. Finally Cole unpinned the note and with a trembling hand he gave it to Pops. Even the note was covered in blood. Pops understood in an instant. Madeline had named her daughter. '*Her name is Paradise.*'

"Pops help me. What will I do? I don't know how to raise a kid without my Madeline. Is this kid the reason Madeline is dead?"

Pops gently took the baby from Cole. "She has a name, Cole. Your wife wanted it that way. Call your daughter by her name."

Very quietly, speaking directly to the child, Pops said, "We know, little one, we know. *Your name is Paradise.* Your mother has given you a beautiful name and introduced you to us. Welcome my darlin' child. We love you already."

Pops placed Paradise on a clean blanket on the floor and whispered to Cole that he would walk down to the docks and ask someone to call the undertaker. And the doctor too. Yes, Pops wanted to know why Madeline was dead. They needed answers. He would get mad and sad tomorrow.

Today it was all about Paradise.

12
1979

As Pops sat on the dock looking directly into her eyes he knew Paradise was in shock. It was too much – for both of them.

Maybe that was enough for today. This heartbreaking story wasn't going away anytime soon. It didn't need to be told all at once.

Pops tried, once again, to make sure he picked the right words although he didn't know if it was possible to make Paradise feel any worse. He may have rushed the story of her birth and said some things wrong. He was so upset he couldn't even remember everything that had been said. Pops felt he had gone back in time and all he knew for certain was that it was done and he couldn't take it back. He told the story as he remembered it. He knew that didn't mean he said it right.

"Your momma died so you might live, little one. She gave you your name but didn't live long enough to give you anything else. Your momma and daddy didn't know how short their *forever* was goin' to be, darlin', and they were after wantin' so much more for your *forever*. You'll have to trust me Paradise. It's all true."

Wiping his brow Pops went on. "I think that's enough for today, don't you?"

"My dear Pops, I know this hasn't been easy," Paradise began. "Thank you for your honesty. I need to know more, but not today." She felt ill. She felt lonely, yet she felt the need to be alone.

In a daze Paradise rose from her perch on the dock and walked back to her tiny apartment. In her entire life she had never felt worse.

Dead. My mother is dead. God in Heaven, why am I even here? Why did I move to Mavillette if not to meet my mother?

Still fully clothed Paradise crawled into bed anxious for *this* day to be over.

13

I can't stop crying. It seems I'm upset about everything.

It's been raining for days. I've been living exclusively *inside* my tiny apartment, accomplishing nothing, waiting for the sun to come out until Laura, a neighbour, dropped in with coffee. She also arrived armed with a bit of free advice. Laura suggested folks around here don't bother with weather reports unless they're fishermen. "We *live* each day of our lives regardless of the weather and you need to adopt our attitude." Laura went on and made it a bit more personal. "Get off your ass, my dear, and get out of this apartment. I know you love your place but get out. I mean it, Paradise. *Get. Out.*"

I'm trying, but it's hard.

Weeks have passed and I haven't found the courage to return to Cape St Mary. I'm so lost.

My fisherman has so much more to share. I want to know. *I need to know* but I'm not strong enough at the moment. What about my father? Does Pops know where he is? I know he told me Cole is his grandson so where is he and why haven't I seen him? It doesn't speak well for my father that he's letting Pops tell me the story of my birth and his first days with me as an infant. I'm a bit angry with him for leaving this all on Pops' shoulders. I've been singularly focussed on my mother, but knowing she's dead I have to move on and meet my father. I want to meet him *now*.

At the moment, my heart is shattered and I can't seem to get out of my own way. I've become best friends with every Headline News anchor on television, meaning I've literally been sitting at home whenever I'm not at work. I've turned out to be my adoptive mother watching the news all day and all night. What's even worse, I'm doing nothing for myself personally – nothing.

Every night I go to bed promising myself tomorrow will be different. *I will make it different.* I don't.

I'm even watching a daily soap opera on television. My mother loves to watch soap operas. She has a friend who uses an expression something like, 'You'll know when it's Friday because the soap operas always leave you hanging.' I now know that to be true. I hate watching my show on a Friday. I won't be telling too many people about my new best friends. Now *that's* depressing.

I need motivation. I need to look forward not back. I need to work on myself. I can't keep working three jobs and return home at day's end knowing my heart isn't in any of the three. I pretend everything with me is hunky-dory but that's not true.

Until I learned of my birth mother's fate I was doing well with my twice-a-week night classes at the police academy up the line. When I graduate I hope to work for myself as a private investigator so I'm desperate to get back on track and resume my classes. God only knows where I'll get work as a PI but I will. Who says women can't work in policing? If I stay here I know I'll be the first female PI in these parts. I like the sound of that.

Even if I don't have my birth mother I still have my mother in Toronto. It could be a whole lot worse. I've started another letter to Mom – haven't quite finished it yet. I think it would feel good to be in touch on a regular basis.

Mom doesn't know about the police academy. She still isn't keen on the gun stuff so I won't mention it just yet. Dad will be proud of me for being able to shoot a gun if nothing else. I can hear him now. 'I taught her how to shoot a damn gun from the time she was a baby. I taught her everything she knows.'

In truth, Dad loves me in his own way. As a very young child I remember Dad playing games with us and reading to me at night when Mom was busy with Wilmot. As I got older and witnessed his control over my mother, I think I chose to forget some of the good memories we created together.

I really want to do something about the way I look. (I can hardly believe I'm admitting it even to myself.) From the day I left the convent I've pretended that how I look isn't important to me. Not true. I've never in my life had a proper haircut, a pedicure or manicure, a facial or a massage. I can do better.

Growing up in Toronto there were a few places near our home where we could look through the window and watch women having their feet attended to. Even the word pedicure was new to me when Mom first explained why women were sitting with their feet up so someone else could paint their toes. She would say, 'Paradise, let's go see who's getting their feet *prettied-up* today.' Then she would laugh. Mom always reminded me to not stare, which I found funny because staring through the storefront windows was exactly what we did most of the time.

In truth I don't need all of those services. I can do without everything but the haircut. I need my hair styled. Right now my reddish-blonde hair is halfway down my back. I trim it myself.

I'm just over five foot ten and tend to slouch so I seem shorter. I'm slim but think I look too skinny – and on and on it goes. I buy my clothes at Frenchy's so I'm never sure what size I wear because the tags are often missing. When I see labels I look for a size twelve but I suspect I am a couple of sizes smaller than that.

I really am a mess.

I have total confidence in my level of intelligence and my ability to learn so much more. *But confidence in my body – not so much.* I need to start projecting an air of confidence if I'm going to work in law enforcement. Standing up straight would be a good place to start.

I've got that don't-mess-with-me expression down pat and believe it or not I think high-heeled shoes are in my future. Killer high heeled shoes. Maybe red killer high heeled shoes. Stab 'em stilettos might work on the job as well as off the job. Even if the shoes never happen it improves my mood just thinking about it.

Really? Are these *really* my thoughts? Next thing you know I'll decide I'm ready to start dating. (Wearing my red killer high heeled shoes no doubt.) Seems I've started a brouhaha with myself.

I wonder if Thomas ever thinks about the last time he saw me – we were celebrating my sixteenth birthday. He's probably forgotten all about me especially since our date ended abruptly when I tried to explain why I had chosen Him over him. As Thomas walked away from me I silently sang *our* song, 'Save the Last Dance for Me'.

I have thought about our last date so many times. I know Thomas was unprepared for my decision. He was certain I would finish school and become his wife. He was angry when he left me. I should have thought more carefully before I spoke the words that would drive Thomas away from me.

I wonder if Thomas is married? I bet his girlfriend (wife) wears high heeled shoes.

Sometimes I wake up in the morning in my own little world with my own peace and quiet and I think the *best thing* about me is that I'm not married.

Sometimes in the evening I walk home alone from one of my many jobs and I think the *worst thing* about me is that I'm not married.

Conflicted? Seems so.

14
1979

I've been busy these past several months and come *hell or high water* I'm getting on with my life.

My fisherman's name is Alphonse. Yesterday at the coffee shop one of my customers stopped as she was leaving and under her breath said, "Paradise, Alphonse is worried about you."

"I don't know any Alphonse," I quickly replied. Clearly her mission was to fill me in and she had lots to share. She even had notes.

Alphonse had been asking about me for a couple of weeks. He asked my customer if she thought I was sick. She said his exact words were, 'I'm after needin' to know if the little one is okay so can you get a message to her for me? Tell her I'm worried about where she's at. And tell her I'm ready to keep talkin' too. '

I need to face facts and let Alphonse tell me more about my birth and my parents – both of my parents. It's not fair to him that I've been too frightened to return to the pier at Cape St Mary.

I think Alphonse will be proud of what I've been doing though and how I've kept busy. My big news is that I've graduated from the PI Academy and can hang my shingle as they say. My birth mother was a good shot and so am I. I wonder what else we have in common? I'll ask if Pops has any pictures of my parents. I would love to be able to see if there are any similarities in our looks. I've never been able to look at anyone and see a hint of myself – no mirror images for me.

Becoming a PI is a dream come true, and I'm proud of myself. However, before I give up my day jobs I need to find work in my chosen profession. It might not be easy. I definitely need to have my Helen Reddy on.

Part of the *hell or high water* I'm dealing with goes back to my time at the convent – or, more specifically, some of the activities there. I left without confirming any facts even though I saw much of it first-hand.

I didn't know for sure, but I suspected I was pregnant with Thomas's child when I entered the convent. When I was certain that indeed I was pregnant I didn't tell anyone until it became obvious.

I was a mess to put it mildly – and still a kid too. I can recall the desperate feeling of loneliness as I cradled my growing belly while alone in my cell.

I needed to talk about this with Thomas that last night we were together but he got upset so fast I couldn't do it. I wanted to tell him how scared and how worried I was. He *might* become a father – in just over seven months if my calculations were in any way accurate. We would be parents and I would still be only sixteen. I needed his help *then*. It wasn't a storybook ending. Thomas got angry and I got away. End of story. Not really.

As part of my penance for arriving pregnant and hiding it for as long as I did, albeit never explained that way, I was assigned to the birthing room where I would sit with soon-to-be mothers as their child was being delivered. It was news to me that several (more than several if I'm being honest) young women were at the convent solely to have their baby. Becoming a nun was not on their list of things to do. What we *did* have in common was that most were young teenagers like me who were not going to keep their baby. We were giving our babies up for adoption. *We were giving them away.*

Bless me Father for I have sinned.

No outsiders were allowed in the birthing room. Fortunately we did have a Sister who had been a nurse in another life before giving her life to God. Sister Adeline was in charge of all baby deliveries. Thank God for her. She could do the work of many when the process began. She made me dizzy but I liked her very much. Sister would immediately leave the room with the newborn to clean and wrap the baby before returning if that had been pre-arranged. If a new mother was keeping her child or if she had asked to see her baby before giving it up Sister was to make that happen.

Not always, but often, poor Sister Adeline had to come back to the birthing room and explain to a new mother that her baby had died. Sadly, some babies were stillborn and others died just seconds after Sister rushed out of the birthing room. I was glad that wasn't my job. Never once, not for a second, did I think anything illegal was going on. Sometimes as we sat together after evening prayers my friends (*friends on the inside* we liked to say) and I would wonder aloud how it was even possible that so many babies died in our convent. The mothers were so young and so healthy. I knew it didn't add up but at the same time I didn't let my mind go there. It was far too personal for me.

If I liked Sister Adeline before giving birth myself I *loved* her after. She could not have been more gentle or more kind. She knew I was giving my baby up for adoption and that I wanted to hold my baby before she took him or her away. Sister promised I would meet my newborn. I understood adoptions were confidential but again, in my case, Sister made a second promise. She would inform Wilmot when I had successfully given birth and she would also tell him (in confidence obviously – this was a huge thing) *who* had adopted my child. Only my brother would ever know. That's the secret I asked Wilmot to keep. *No one else must ever know – including Thomas. Especially Thomas.*

I dreaded the actual birth and prayed it would be over in seconds. I was more than a little unprepared. After many long hours in labour Sister put my daughter on my chest – even before they cleaned her up. I was in love. She was perfect. Fingers, toes, big eyes (closed for the most part but I could tell they were beautiful big eyes) and the softest skin. In truth her skin was wrinkled beyond belief but it was soft and beautiful just the same.

Tiny fingers gripping mine, I knew every inch of my daughter by the time Sister came to take her away.

She had given me extra time and I was so thankful.

"Thank you so much, Sister Adeline," I said between swallowing my tears. "Thank you for calling my brother with the news and can *I ask one more thing*?"

Sister seemed cross with me as she reached the door in the birthing room and turned to face me. "Paradise, you have already asked me to break the law by telling your brother *who* is adopting your baby – what is it now?"

Her name is Hope. "Please tell them her name is Hope."

***

So many years have passed. My baby girl is almost seven years old. *Where are you, Hope?*

15
1980

I forgot to give her the dried fish last time. Damn near talked Paradise into an early grave by the look on her face when she left me that day. I think I went too far – shouldn't have told her that her mom was dead the way I did. Wish I was better with my words. My Cole was some good with words.

When is a good time to tell someone his or her mother is dead? Everyone knows the answer to that. Never. I'm after doin' a better job tellin' her what happened when I talk about my Cole. God help me the day I have to share that story.

Sittin' here on the pier I'm hopin' today's not the day. She's walkin' my way and she's determined. I can see it in her walk. I wonder if the Academy helped with her confidence? I won't tell her I know anything about that. Paradise can shoot a gun like a man – just like her mom. I couldn't be more proud.

"Sorry I've been missing in action, Alphonse. Is it all right if I call you Alphonse?"

"Well, that's better than callin' me 'sir', Paradise. Look at us. On a first-name basis." Trying to keep it light Alphonse rose and tentatively reached out to offer a hug.

"I'm real sorry about your mom. She was one strong woman and I know you are too. How much more do you want to know today?"

"Can I share some news first, Alphonse? It's really big news actually. I've just graduated from the PI Academy. Not sure if you heard." Giving him no chance to comment Paradise went on. "I've been shooting a gun since I was a kid. My dad, well my dad in Toronto I mean, taught me to shoot which made that part of my training the easiest." Seeing the worried look on his face Paradise added, "Don't worry Alphonse. I'm hoping shooting my gun won't happen with every case I'm on."

Without admitting he already heard her good news Alphonse asked if Paradise had any PI related work coming her way since her graduation. He wanted to help. "I have to say, I'm hopin' you get lots of work that doesn't involve *ever* drawin' that gun of yours. Maybe you could stay safe and rescue cats or somethin'." They shared an easy laugh before getting back on topic.

"Seriously, Paradise, we grow more than fishermen here in Cape St Mary. I can put in a good word with a few of my fisherman friends. Some of my buddies have family in your line of work. Curtis is a policeman right here and Clint is a PI in Ontario. I fish with their granddads.

"Clint works with a third PI who lives in another country they tell me. I know nothin' about him other than he's got more trainin' than both Curtis and Clint. Seems strange to me Clint can do *real work* with a PI who works somewhere else. Maybe I'm just getting too old to understand it all. Shouldn't they be in the same place to do good work?"

He'd forgotten about the dried fish again. "Are you after eatin' dried fish, Paradise? I brought you some last time but got lost in tellin' you about your mom and forgot to give it to you."

"I love dried fish. Thank you for thinking of me."

They talked for hours about PI work and how Paradise might be able to give up one maybe two of her current jobs *if* she could get a bit of PI work locally.

Paradise wasn't ready to tell Alphonse about her brother's disappearance and how she hoped to use some of her new PI skills to find him. She knew she would have to spend time in Toronto to work on Wilmot's case and she was prepared to do that. She would explain another day.

Names for her little business were tossed around and after much discussion they agreed on Paradise Pu'olo. Pu'olo is the Hawaiian word for package and given that Paradise was open to travel and Hawaii was right up there on her list of places to visit, it was official. Paradise Pu'olo would go on her business cards when she had time to find a printing place. Might have to head up the line for that.

"Paradise, this afternoon with you feels like a gift you've given an old man. Let's call it a day – a day of lookin' forward, not back. Lots of time to tell you the rest of the story about how you ended up livin' in Toronto after the first three years of your life here with us. Okay by you?"

"Sure is. Thanks for listening to me, Alphonse, and thanks for caring about my future too."

The old fisherman thought for a long minute before he spoke again. "One more thing Paradise. A favour really. You can call me Alphonse if you want, but I think I would like to be Pops to you just like I was to your mother. Could you handle that?"

Not wanting to end another day together in tears Paradise kept it light. "Roger that, Pops. See you next time."

Pops watched Paradise slowly stand and turn to walk home. With a smile on her face, the wind at her back and a future taking shape he felt his love for her grow. When she stopped to wave one more time Pops could see she was already munching on the dried fish. "Well, I'll be damned," Pops muttered as he made his own way down the pier. "So like her mother. God willin', she might even call this place home for good." He had a few calls to make to get some work thrown her way.

A perfect day just happened.
Been a long time since a perfect day.
Since my Cole.

16
1981

Marie knew she still had considerable work to do. Her body was responding but not her mind. *She simply could not remember.* Certainly not fast enough. Living in a hospital-like setting God knows where, Marie knew she had to face another day. Her nurse would be here soon.

Marie liked her nurse. There were others, but she thought of Mary Rose as her own private nurse. When she arrived here by ambulance Mary Rose was the first nurse she met. Funny how she could remember meeting her nurse yet she remembered so little about her life prior to that day. "You're safe and well cared for and that's all you need to know for now, my dear." Mary Rose sat with Marie that first day and continued to reinforce all they could do to help her. "Everything will come back to you in time, Marie. Let's ensure your bones are well healed before we seriously work on your memory and any other emotional issues you face. Your bones *must* heal first. You've been to death's door and back. I'm here to help you day in and day out." Her nurse didn't want Marie to worry about anything. "You're exactly where you need to be. Let *us* do the worrying dear."

There were days Marie didn't even know *who* she was. Every day was spent trying to remember.

Marie did have one vivid and violent memory. It haunted her dreams. It was always the same and it came to her every night.

Someone came to my apartment. He said he worked for Meat. He came with a message that Meat was busy with Wilmot so had sent him to remind me of a few things. I don't recall what he said after that but I do remember one very hard kick to my body. I wasn't expecting it and wasn't prepared so I didn't even try to protect myself. The kick was followed by another and another. My nurses have told me there were many kicks, most of them to my head, and perhaps it was best that I didn't remember all of the details.

Who's Meat and who's Wilmot? I ask myself the same question every morning when I wake up. Whoever beat me didn't tell me his name but he did make sure I heard their names.

As Mary Rose opened the curtains in her room Marie's concentration was broken. The work to restore more of her memory would continue once she was up and ready to face her physiotherapy for the day. Once her physio was behind her each day she moved on to the real work with yet another therapist. *The real work was getting her memory back and not losing her mind in the process.* There were days Marie felt like giving up but Mary Rose was always there to calm her down.

Marie desperately wanted to remember everything Meat's man had told her. The words were hiding somewhere in the back of her mind. Marie could feel the words, she just couldn't grab them.

The police hoped Marie would recover and be able to answer some questions. Someone had made the phone call hours, possibly minutes, after she was badly beaten. They found her lying in her own blood with a faint pulse and the most vacant of eyes. She was near death. An ambulance rushed her to the hospital where, over many months, Marie faced numerous surgeries and a lengthy stay. Next step for Marie had been an isolated long-term facility where the real work began.

Years passed. Recovery, both physical and mental, was slow but steady.

"Good morning, my dear." Marie turned slowly to face Mary Rose and another day. "Look out the window, Marie. It's beautiful outside. Your morning is already half-finished so let's not waste another second with you in this bed. Do you think you can stand up for me again today, Marie? Hold my arm. You did so well yesterday – today is a brand new experience for us. Come on now, let's see what we can do." Marie sat up, willed her tiny legs over the side of the bed, took a deep breath and smiled at her nurse. Mary Rose held her hand out to Marie. *"Hold on to me."*

For a split-second Marie caught a glimpse of a former life. A kind man had helped her. She couldn't picture his face but she remembered him speaking to her.

"Hold on Marie, help is coming. Hold on to me." Marie thought she remembered this man leaving her before help arrived. But, why would he leave her if she had been badly beaten? In that split-second she had remembered something new and it made her happy. Marie wasn't often happy. Most of all she remembered him saying, *"I love you, Marie. Never forget that."*

Marie hoped her therapist could help her remember more when they had their session after lunch. She wasn't always eager to meet her therapist because she rarely had anything new to share. She could picture the delight on her therapist's face when she began today's session with, *"Doctor, I have wonderful news. I remember – someone loved me."*

Part Three

Pd – Private Investigator

17
1981

There were no female officers with the local police force and Sergeant Curtis felt this case could benefit from a woman's touch. Pd, as she was known to everyone, was doing him a favour. She was giving it *her* touch.

Sergeant Curtis was doing Pd a favour as well. She was a local private investigator and without much work in this small community he didn't mind throwing a case or two her way. Old man and everyone's favourite fisherman from Cape St Mary, Alphonse d'Entremont, spoke with Curtis about Paradise and her chosen career. Curtis was eager to help. He hadn't met Paradise yet but with all the positive comments Alphonse had to share Curtis was anxious to meet her. Alphonse didn't often ask for a favour so when he did, everyone listened. "She's just after needin' a bit of experience to add to her résumé, or whatever you folks call it, that's all," was how Alphonse explained it. Enough said.

Watching two wide-eyed teenagers through the one-way glass in the interrogation room of the local precinct, Pd could, just for a moment, see them as innocents. Seeing them as murderers was more than a bit difficult. Morning Glory and Dawn were the only names these shivering teens would give and for now they were getting away with it.

Had they been in the wrong place at the wrong time or did one of these young women actually own a gun? Hard to imagine this happening in a clothing store given these two were certainly under-dressed. Or, *hardly dressed at all,* Paradise thought. Little bloody wonder they were shivering.

Listening to Morning Glory and Dawn and their never-ending story, Pd decided it was time to get involved. Her locked-and-loaded stance wasn't required on this particular day but she wore it anyway. If her instructors at the PI academy had demonstrated the locked-and-loaded stance once they had demonstrated it a million times. Standing tall, Pd entered the interrogation room and took a seat facing the prisoners. That's what Curtis had called them when he requested her help. Said there had been a shooting at a clothing store in nearby Digby and these two women had been identified as the shooters. Curtis gave her a nod and left the room.

Paradise thought she would ask a personal question or two first. Once she established a comfortable connection she would get down to business. The conversation didn't go as she planned.

"Where do you live, ladies?"

"Wherever we want. Any more questions, bitch?"

"Let's try that again. Where do you live, ladies?"

"We need some water or something."

Pd ignored their request.

"Would you like to call your parents?"

"Ah, that would be pair-ants in our case. They're ants. Nothing but ants under our feet. We would step on them both if they walked in here, which they won't. We know nothing about them and they know the same about us. Keeping it that way will make sure we don't get no more hurt. We want it left that way."

Pd took her time getting the girls a drink. She needed to think. That last tirade by the smaller of the two girls spoke volumes. They may be sisters in crime. They may be estranged from their parents. Or they may have fallen in with the wrong crowd. Dear God in heaven what have these young girls been exposed to?

Time to try again.

"I understand you've both declined the opportunity to make your one call. There is no one you want to contact. Is this correct?"

"Hmmm, let me see," said Morning Glory once again with her stage face on. "Do you by chance know any nine-millimetre Glocks who might be able to help us bust out of this dump you call a lock-up? Glocks talk real loud. Know what I mean, Miss-fancy-pants-private-investigator?"

This was getting Pd nowhere. Opening the door she asked Curtis to join them. "Give the girls a room for the night, Sergeant. Put them together for now. Maybe a good catnap on a bad cot will help our guests be a bit more talkative in the morning."

Turning back to the girls, Pd lowered her voice. "Sleep tight, ladies, and remember someone is *dead* and *you* are our prime suspects. I'll be back in the morning and when I walk in here there will be no more jokes." Slamming both fists on the desk as she stood up Pd walked out.

Holding the girls might not be the right thing to do. Pd was missing something. Why the phony names and why the bad attitude? Couldn't they see they were in trouble and she wanted to help? Pd wanted to be on their side. Life always seemed to *blame the girl* and she would not do that without facts. At the moment she had none.

Draining her very cold and very stale coffee, Pd allowed her mind to wander back to a time when she too was a teenager.

She wondered what happened to him. Her Elvis. Her Thomas.

Thomas had been her first I'm-attracted-to-a-boy feeling. He made her feel special from her thirteenth birthday until this very day, even with so many years separating them now. The memory of Thomas haunted her at the strangest of times.

With all of her heart Pd hoped Wilmot had kept his promise and not shared her secret with Thomas.

18

'No one can make you feel inferior without your consent.' If the quote is good enough for Eleanor Roosevelt, it's good enough for me, thought Paradise as she sifted through her notes hours after returning home from the police station and her first encounter with Morning Glory and Dawn.

Paradise was second-guessing herself. Her mind was all over the map. The facts were not lining up. She drove directly from the police station to the crime scene only to see the yellow tape in the garbage and staff preparing to open the doors to the public in the morning. Maybe she was new to policing but she knew this crime scene had *not* been protected. When a murder is committed the yellow tape stays in place until all evidence is collected and all questions have been answered. *Especially a murder scene.* Paradise wasn't the only one who had lots to learn. She would discuss this with Sergeant Curtis at a later date.

Time to stop feeling inferior. She could figure this out. A man was dead and someone had murdered him.

Before leaving the station, Curtis asked if Pd wanted to see photos of the crime scene. Little did she know what the camera had captured. The deceased, for some yet unexplained reason, had died with his penis exposed. This, of course, was the talk of the town or at least the talk of everyone who had been in the store at the time and within the viewing area. The poor man had a name, and someone had given his penis a name too – Mr Happy. There had been more discussion about Mr Happy than his face or the identification found on the body. Pd knew the man didn't deserve the verbal exchange. What about his poor family?

Paradise chose not to mention she hadn't seen many Mr Happys in her lifetime. Being a nun doesn't lend itself to penis viewing. She didn't realize, and at first didn't understand, names are sometimes assigned to a penis when the occasion fits. When she first entered the police station and heard officers talking about Mr Happy, Paradise assumed this was the victim's name. Honestly. The joke was on her.

Crucial facts of a case are sometimes leaked to the local media and this concerned Paradise. Media can be cruel especially if too many details leak out. Mr Happy, for example. Paradise might even know the widow of the deceased. Maybe she waits on her at the coffee shop. Paradise liked to think she could be of some help to her. She made a mental note to check into this once the case was solved. For now though, she had work to do.

Police training makes it clear that keeping the proper distance from the victim and certainly from the accused is important. Help them but don't be their friend. Paradise knew she would have to keep this in mind. She had been told repeatedly during mock exercises that she was not doing well disassociating herself from the victim, the victim's family and, yes, sometimes the accused as well. This was an essential part of the job. Being a people person is apparently not always a good thing.

Reviewing her checklist of facts as well as her new list of questions to be asked, Paradise was anxious for night to pass. She wanted to return to the police station and see how Morning Glory and Dawn were doing in the cold harsh light of day.

Midnight arrived and passed as Paradise continued to study the facts of the case. Sleep evaded her. Still wide awake.

'Pair-ants' the girls had called their parents. What was that about? Paradise was shocked when the girls declined the opportunity to make a phone call from lock-up. She wondered what the relationship with their parents must be like. She hoped they would reconsider and ask to make that call when she returned to the police station in the morning.

Finally, it was time to force herself to call it a day. Sleep on it so to speak. Hopefully morning would bring clarity. It was already three a.m. so if she didn't sleep soon there would be none at all.

Paradise awoke in a panic. She had forgotten to call someone to cover her shift at the coffee shop. She was going to be a *real* private investigator today but she couldn't afford to neglect any of the jobs that paid her bills.

"Not to worry," Alan said when Paradise called her boss at the café. "Curtis was in for a late-night coffee and told us you were on a case so we covered your shift for today and tomorrow too. You do what you've trained to do. We're all real proud of you, Paradise. By the way, I hear they call you 'Pd' down at the station. I like it."

Alan was a good friend to Paradise and to Pops as well. She suspected Pops might have also been in on the conversation they had last night.

After a quick shower Paradise braided her long hair and made a mental note to book that appointment to have a real stylist work some magic with her hair.

Giving it some thought Paradise decided to pack her gun, now tucked neatly and safely into her shoulder strap. Likely she wouldn't need it today but you never know. She would have her gun with her at all times when doing PI work so she might as well get used to it.

Gun in place, she slipped her denim jacket on, put her today-list in her pocket and what the heck – she applied a bit of lip-gloss too.

Wearing lip-gloss was new to Paradise. It added a bit of fun to her life as pathetic as that sounded even to her. She might want to reapply it at some point during the day so she tucked the tube into her pocket. Until now Paradise had not given much thought to her appearance. That was changing. Baby steps.

Morning shift and Pd was going to work.

19

Pops knew Paradise wouldn't be meeting him on the dock anytime soon. She landed a case with Sergeant Curtis and work would definitely come first. "I'm after bein' real happy about that to be honest," Pops said out loud to no one in particular. He did a bit of bragging about Paradise with the boys on the pier, but they were all out fishing so he had the dock to himself in the early morning mist on this particular day. He hadn't told anyone about their real connection yet. That would be a story for Paradise to tell.

Pops knew the history these two shared would shock more than a few people. A welcomed shock, he hoped.

When they did find time to talk, Pops would pick his story up where he and Cole learned how to care for an infant. They had to dry their tears pretty fast and get on with feeding, clothing and learning what each different cry meant. This baby sure did keep two fishermen on their toes.

We were learnin' fast and lovin' every second of it. Paradise will be proud of her daddy when I finish sharin' the story.

Talk at the coffee shop last night had upset Pops. Curtis was saying he brought Paradise in because he thought the case needed a woman's touch. "Isn't that damn near as bad as me sayin' she shoots like a man?" If it wasn't right to suggest a woman who is a good shot is shooting like a man, how can it be okay to say a case needs a woman's touch? "I'm too old to understand this woman doin' a man's job stuff," Pops said. "Paradise has landed me right in the middle of it so I reckon I better get learnin' fast."

Colour me confused. Pops heard Paradise use that expression one day and he liked it. He needed a few new words and some of her words rolled around in his mouth real nice.

20

A coffee run might be a good idea. Not knowing how the girls in lock-up or the officers at the station liked their coffee, Paradise ordered an even dozen cups of black coffee. She brought milk, cream and sugar from home. With full hands she entered the police station.

"Heads up if you want coffee," Paradise said to no one in particular. She was unprepared for the comments that followed.

"Oh. My. God. You brought us coffee? Marry me, Pd."

"I love you, Pd."

"Can I take you home tonight?"

"What are you hiding under that long hair, girl?"

"Pd, where have you been all my life?"

Good thing the officers didn't know that not only was Paradise a former nun but comments like these had never been thrown her way, even as a joke. *Dear Lord in heaven, couldn't they just thank me for the coffee and leave it at that?* Interesting way to start the day.

Small talk was foreign to Paradise so she changed the subject by asking for the status on Morning Glory and Dawn. "Anything happen during the night? Did the girls say anything or ask for anything?" No one seemed to know. Curtis was out interviewing someone related to the case but no one had details. They would have to wait for his return to see if there had been any developments.

"Okay, boys, I'm taking three cups of coffee with me and will keep you posted. Leave us alone and if Sergeant Curtis comes in, ask him to trust me. I have an idea and he is *not* to interrupt us."

The comments continued as Paradise walked away. Comments having nothing to do with the case – or the coffee.

"How tall is she, boys? Six feet?"

"How come we know absolutely nothing about Pd anyway?"

"I'm guessin' lots of our local gals are jealous of this tall drink of water. All I know is she's taller than my woman and my woman is *tall*!"

"Rumour has it our little gal comes from the NYPD *not* from the PI academy up the line. My wife heard she had an affair with a police officer in the higher up ranks and that's how she was able to get her PI training so fast."

"Your wife's jealous of her, pal."

Then came the most interesting comment of all (clearly they didn't realize she could still hear them). "My wife thinks Paradise has a bit of a strange and murky past. I wouldn't mind getting murky with our very own Pd."

Strange and murky indeed.

Paradise had brought more than coffee for the girls. Her back-pack was full of clothes because, in her opinion, they were practically naked when they were brought in. How could a woman willingly dress like that? It seemed to Paradise they were more undressed than dressed.

If her learning curve was this steep in life and with every PI job she took on, she was in for quite an education. Where do women buy clothes like the skimpy things on these two girls? Not from Frenchy's, that's for sure. Paradise thought she had seen it all with some of the nearly-not-there bras and panties she handled as she sorted clothing for the many bins at the local Frenchy's. A different bin for each size, shape and style – practically every item of clothing you could imagine.

Paradise and her co-workers at Frenchy's often put clothes aside to chat about during their breaks. They called these skimpy items 'nearly-nots' and always had a good laugh pretending they were going to take the items home and wear them. Not likely – at least in her case.

21

Entering the cell with an intended silence Paradise was struck by the difference in the demeanour of both girls. Standing but slouching rather than shoulders back, chest out and chin up as they had been yesterday Paradise knew she had been correct to give the girls the night in lock-up to *think about things*. Morning Glory was pouting. Dawn was crying. In the cold harsh light of day they looked like kids. She was anxious to learn how old these girls were.

Without saying a word, Paradise held out two cups of hot coffee – willingly accepted with a smile and a soft, "Thank you," from Dawn. Morning Glory accepted her coffee with nothing more than a nod. Paradise opened her backpack and offered one-size-fits-all sweatshirts and oversized sweatpants. Nothing matched. Didn't matter. Both girls quickly grabbed the clothing and began to dress, putting their new clothes over what they were already wearing. She knew they were both more comfortable now even if they couldn't, or wouldn't, admit it.

Paradise decided to try breaking the ice by approaching this as three girls simply having a conversation rather than two girls plus a PI. She knew she should stay away from a personal discussion but dove in anyway.

"Just out of curiosity, where in God's good name do you buy your underwear which, by the way, is about all you had on when you were arrested. I know you were shopping but unless you stripped in the aisles to try something on I can't imagine why you were dressed that way."

"Can you say Victoria's Secret?" came the reply. "And, yes we like to dress this way. Well, maybe not quite this way but we were trying to impress someone and we know he likes girls to wear Victoria's Secret *all the time*. He's a good guy who's helping us look for work around here."

"Victoria's what?" Paradise was rewarded with a genuine laugh from both of the girls.

"Have you not heard of Victoria's Secret? Where does your man buy your clothes?"

"I hate to break it to you, girls, but what you came in wearing last night didn't leave much room for secrets of any kind." She ignored their second question.

Time to go to work. "Ladies, I have asked the officers on duty to leave us alone for awhile. We need to talk and I need some truthful answers. Tell me what you know about the shooter and the poor sod that was murdered. Tell me *everything* so I can help you. How old are you for starters?"

The girls looked first at each other and then at Paradise. It seemed Dawn would do the talking for both of them, at least in the beginning. Dawn appeared the more dominant of the two and Paradise could see she had something to say. The girls exchanged eye contact as Dawn began.

"Our lives have been pande-fucking-monium since we arrived here two days ago. We don't know a thing about whatever happened at that store yesterday." After a pause to take another gulp of coffee she continued. "Look, we met this guy in Toronto and he told us we were real pretty and we could make tons of money if we wanted to be dancers. He was from down here somewhere and we had just gotten into a bad fight with our parents and when he said we could drive here with him in his van we thought it was a great idea. At the time." Dawn couldn't stop talking and she spoke in very long sentences. "He was helping us pick out some clothes and he's the one who told us we should be real proud of our bodies and if we wanted to prove to him that we could dance in public we needed to strip down right there in the store and try on whatever he threw at us." Morning Glory put her hand over her sister's mouth. "I think you've said enough, dear. That's more than I thought you were going to share. We might get in trouble."

"You *might* get in trouble?" Paradise could not believe her ears. "Do you even *begin* to understand the trouble you're in? Someone fired a gun from the area of the store where you were standing and witnesses say *no*

118

one else was nearby. Look at me, girls. Someone is dead. D.E.A.D."

Morning Glory appeared frozen to the floor. She seemed to be batting at imaginary flies around her face. There were no flies. Paradise knew it was nerves and decided to turn her line of questioning to Morning Glory to see if she would share more information.

Dawn clearly had more control of her emotions at the moment. Paradise reached out to take Morning Glory's hand. Shoulders shaking as she began to cry, Morning Glory crumbled. At first she couldn't speak.

"Let it all out. Tell me everything beginning with your ages. You've avoided that question long enough."

"Dawn is almost seventeen, okay, so please let her go home. No, let her go somewhere so she can be safe. She won't want to go home. I'll stay here if you want but my sister is a kid. Please help her. I'll do anything you say. I'm begging you to help my sister. Just tell me what to do."

"And how old are you, Morning Glory?"

Head almost on her chest she whispered, "I'm nearly eighteen. I should know better. We set out to be better than our parents. We have always been alone and we needed food so we had to quit school and look for work and don't even get me started on how we ended up thinking about being dancers."

"Yes," Dawn wanted to chime in. "And now here we are in this godforsaken place. I need to get out of here, bitch. Please. Please. Please." Her control vanished and clearly she had reverted back to yesterday's child. She was playing the part of the wanna-be dancer in lock-up. Paradise didn't believe it.

"Calling me a bitch while you're saying please is not a good way to get me to help you, Dawn. Settle down. *Now*."

The girls did settle down and hours passed as they shared the details, as their young minds understood them, surrounding how they were picked up in Toronto, driven to Digby and then ended up in the clothing store when the shooting took place. It seemed they were looking for *work* clothes.

Once the girls were drained of all knowledge that might help, Paradise left them to fill Curtis in. She was certain Morning Glory and Dawn were picked up by a pimp who brought them here to dance/strip/prostitute themselves, or at the very least to be trained in the profession before moving on to larger centers. *I would love to come face to face with their pimp Paradise thought.*

"Good work, Pd," said Curtis. "This is valuable information. See if Morning Glory and Dawn can tell you anything else before we're finished with them. The boys and I will get to work on this shortly. We may be out of the station for the rest of the day but not until I get a few more things done here."

Paradise wondered if this is how it would be. The boys go after the killers while the girls stay warm and talk among themselves.

Paradise decided to let the young women cool off for a short time before re-joining them. She felt they might benefit from talking in private. They had shared lots of new information and she was pleased with how she managed the conversation. Her training was being put to good use today.

There was always paperwork to be done. Paperwork would not be the most exciting part of being a private investigator but Paradise tackled it for over an hour before going back to the girls.

Morning Glory and Dawn were sitting patiently. They had already told her everything they could think of that might clear their names. Just as Paradise was asking the girls to share the history behind their names, Curtis rushed into the room, filling it with his presence.

"It's over, Pd. We caught the shooter. He confessed. Two pimps fighting over the girls. Both pimps were armed. One clearly drew his weapon faster than the other." Curtis added the last bit of information with more than a little sarcasm. "The girls can go home or wherever. I don't care. We don't need either of them. Leave the rest of the paperwork to me."

How sensitive of him, Paradise thought. Just like that he turned his back on the young girls. Yesterday he was so eager to lay blame. Today it's all about getting rid of them.

Mother of God. Doesn't anyone care about these two underaged waifs? Paradise wondered if anyone even missed them, *anyone at all.* She decided to take a chance and do something she may have no control over in the end. *Something her training taught her she should never do.*

"How would you girls like to come home with me for the few days you have left here? I'll drive you to the airport when you're ready to return to Toronto but for now you could help me find some nice clothes. What do you say? My place is pretty small but you're welcome to anything I have."

"Actually we *could* help you in the fashion department," Dawn offered with a smile. "You need a lot of work and you need a bit of make-up too. Have you ever heard of make-up?" The girls were enjoying this. "I hate to say this but have you been living under a rock?"

For a moment Morning Glory and Dawn sounded like the young girls they were – all about makeup and clothing.

Dawn went on. "But, honey, we can't turn you in to a dancer. You haven't got the body by the looks of what I can see under those clothes. It's kind of hard to tell with what you're wearing but we don't think you have the curves to be a dancer. Men like their women to have curves. At least the ones who dance for them."

"Public dancing is not on my list of things to do so perhaps not qualifying would be a good thing, girls."

The officers didn't look twice as Paradise led the girls out of the precinct and over to her car. Either they didn't recognize Morning Glory and Dawn in their sweatpants or they had forgotten about them already. All three made a clean escape.

With a smug smile Paradise said, "Some men can be idiots, girls. You should never have been locked up in the first place. That much I know."

22

Janis Ian wrote the song 'At Seventeen' in 1975 while Paradise was tucked away in the convent. It was one of the first songs she heard when she returned to the safety of her bedroom in her parents' home in Toronto. While she didn't feel the song was written for her specifically, she could identify with much of it and the words were running through her head as she woke up.

To those of us who weren't selected for any sports' teams and to those of us who watched the mail for that Valentine that never came. A true-to-life song in so many ways, thought Paradise, as she got out of bed while listening to see if Morning Glory and Dawn had stirred in the next room. She hadn't heard a peep out of them during the night so it was safe to assume they both had a good night's sleep. They would have needed it. Was it possible that she smelled coffee brewing? That would be a first in her apartment unless she made it herself.

Paradise opened her bedroom door and was greeted by two young women she hardly recognized. Freshly scrubbed faces void of all make-up – and there had been tons of makeup. Both girls wore big grins that seemed to say, "We're proud of ourselves this morning."

Paradise looked around her tiny apartment and thought it was cleaner at that moment than it had been since she moved in. The sleeping bags offered last night were neatly rolled up and stacked in the corner of the living room, which was pretty much the entire living area. Yesterday's dirty dishes had been washed and placed in the strainer beside the sink. Three clean cups sat on the counter awaiting that first morning coffee. Paradise could *feel* the beginning of a good day...

All this before eight a.m. Paradise was sure the girls were not used to getting up early *any* morning. This must seem like the middle of the night to them. Before she could speak Dawn held out her hand to silence her. "Let me introduce us to you, Paradise. I'm Mary and this is my little sister Margaret Ville. We want you to know our real names. We are *not* Morning Glory and Dawn. "

Paradise choked back tears and forced herself to not hug them both. It didn't seem the girls were ready for hugs just yet. She had sensed last evening as she brought them to her apartment they needed their distance. Understandably so.

To lighten the mood Paradise spoke next. "I am happy to meet you both. Coffee, please. *Please*."

Mary (Dawn) continued, "Paradise I need to start telling you what we want you to know about us. We decided after you went to bed last night that we were going to be totally honest with you – about everything. Our mother called herself an exotic dancer. She was a stripper, Paradise. There, I said it. I had to get that out.

We know that doesn't make it right for us to do the same thing though.

"We also know we wouldn't have ended up just dancing. We would have been strippers and God knows what else and our booker likely wasn't a booker at all. Like you said, he's a pimp. We're ashamed of ourselves."

It was young Margaret's turn. "Our stripper mother went to prison. We don't know why but we can guess. Our father took us out of school all the time, Paradise. He said it was time we started helping out with paying the bills. He's a drunk, Paradise, and he has done terrible things to us. Selling us to a pimp would only be one of the bad things he has done. We don't really want to say any more right now. Our parents are pair-ants to us."

"Let's not call them pair-ants, girls." Paradise didn't like the expression. "No matter what, they're your parents. We can talk more about that another time but for now drop the expression. Can you do that for me?"

"Consider it dropped. One more thing we want to say though is *thank you* for bringing us to your place and offering to help us. No one has e*ver* done that. We couldn't believe it when you asked us to come home with you last night and then you even gave us a place to sleep. After you being so good to us and all we feel bad for saying you don't know how to dress. We're both sorry for kind of making fun of you."

"Well," began Paradise, "that's quite a lot to take in. I did give you my old sleeping bags but you had to sleep on my floor so I don't think you have to thank me for much. And I'm the one thanking you for cleaning up this morning and making the coffee." Paradise figured the girls were trying to process everything so she gave them a moment.

"Speaking of coffee, seconds anyone? As for my fashion sense, or lack of, perhaps we could talk about that over breakfast."

Silence followed as kitchen contents were mulled over. *No food in this kitchen.* Before Paradise was out of bed the girls had already seen her bare cupboards. "We kind of figured you don't know how to cook anything. There is *no* food here – only coffee stuff," said Margaret.

"You got me. Why don't I take you out for breakfast? That's been my plan since we got up by the way. We can eat at my coffee shop. You can meet my friends and see where I work when I am not being a PI."

Feeling somewhat reflective as she drained her coffee cup Paradise added, "I'll let you in on a little secret, girls. The last two days were my first as a PI and meeting the two of you is the highlight of my last few months."

"Mother of God, you need a life," whispered Mary with a smile. Margaret added, "Yeah, Paradise, you need a life. *Bad.*"

Paradise dug into her Frenchy's bin and gave the girls a few choices of clothing they could wear for the day's adventure. They both selected extremely baggy clothes. This was a bit of a surprise to Paradise albeit she did suspect they were not all that comfortable dressing so everyone could ogle their bodies and comment on their youth. She couldn't begin to imagine what their earlier years had been like at the hands of parents who possibly weren't really equipped to be parents to either of the girls.

Heading for the car Margaret put her hand on Paradise's shoulder and said, "Here, Paradise. For God's sake, put on a bit of lipstick."

This was going to be fun. Paradise would learn as much if not more today than her two guests. She wondered how many times Margaret and Mary had been victims. They were so young and had already seen the underbelly of life in a way she had not experienced. That would come with time and definitely in her newly chosen profession. She knew though, without a doubt, she would never be the victim.

Paradise wanted the girls' 'At Seventeen' experience to be so much better than her own. She knew she could help. She also knew she was getting too close. She reminded herself *once again* she had been warned that in policing it's important to never get involved personally with those you have interviewed behind bars. *Especially* those you have seen behind bars. *Too late.*

Her first job with the local police detachment had happened for a reason – a reason stronger than merely giving her a bit of work and some experience to add to her almost barren resume.

Turning into Pd when she had her PI hat on was working just fine for Paradise. She liked the transition.

23

"Your car looked different in the dark last night, Paradise. Is this the same car?" Before Mary could go on with what Paradise suspected would have been less than a positive comment her sister interrupted.

"And it's a great car. We're happy to have a ride in it, aren't we, Mary?"

"Sure."

"Hey, I'm proud of this car I'll have you know. I bought it myself and paid with cash. It's my *tank*. I need both sides of the road due to the size of it but not to worry. I'll get us to the coffee shop in one piece."

Many people believe I arrived here with a driver's license. Not so. A friend drove with me so I could attend all of my classes at the Police Academy. We stuck to back roads, and I was behind the wheel. When I was ready, we went to Middleton and I took my driver's test there. I didn't know anyone in Middleton and I was anxious to keep the actual date of my driver's test a secret. When I drove this car off the used car lot no one asked a single question. I needed wheels to be a PI.

"What kind of a car is this?"

"It's an Oldsmobile something-or-other with exactly 154,333 miles on it. I don't trust it enough to drive it too far. It does have a pretty good radio so let's see if we can catch a song we like." Paradise wondered if the girls enjoyed music as much as she did. Within seconds Margaret chimed in singing at the top of her lungs, "*Just get on that bus or train, whatever! And no talking...*" they were laughing. The song hadn't been out long and even with the age differences they were all familiar with it. Music brings people together and that was certainly true today.

"Fifty ways to leave your lover." If they only knew, thought Paradise. Maybe later today she would tell them where she had lived from ages sixteen to twenty-one. Wouldn't that be an interesting conversation. They pulled in to the parking lot and got out of the tank.

"Welcome to Cafe Central, ladies. Let's eat." Sliding into one of the booths, Paradise tried to imagine Cafe Central through their eyes and wondered if Mary and Margaret appreciated the extent to which circa 1960s had been respected here. Red vinyl upholstered booths, aluminum napkin dispensers, a jukebox at every table, plastic coated menus and mustard and ketchup at the ready. The girls may be too young to take in the retro but they did seem to like it. They buried their heads in the menu.

"My treat, remember? Eat up. You only get one hot meal a day under my watch and this is it so don't hold back." Paradise suspected the girls had not eaten in some time and not properly in an even longer time.

Consuming a tuna melt, eggs over easy with bacon, French toast with a fruit salad, cold slaw, fries and numerous cups of coffee the girls ate every morsel. They ate from their own plate and from each other's while playing songs on their mini jukebox. When they thought they were full they decided on dessert. Something chocolate. Lots of chocolate.

Out of the corner of his eye Pops was watching. He wondered who the young girls were as he sat quietly on a stool at the counter, trying to get up the nerve to approach their booth.

He wanted to say hi. Or maybe he just wanted to be included. Finally, he caught Paradise's eye.

"Hey, Pops, I didn't see you there," Paradise called out. "Come on over here and meet my friends." Unfortunately, Pops opened his mouth a bit too soon – even before he reached their booth.

"What happened to your case, Paradise? Didn't you have your PI hat on for a day or more?" His line of questioning wasn't over yet and Paradise was too stunned to interrupt. This was not the Pops she knew. "Curtis was after givin' you a good opportunity with this case and from what I hear down on the dock, those two girls are bad and they were the shooters. Are they still in jail? Who's questioning them this morning? Sounds like they're guilty of murder to me and to everyone else around here." As his mouth let him go on and on Pops' mind was thinking something else. *Oh no – is it possible these two girls are the ones I'm speakin' so bad about? Paradise is going to be some mad at me.* He stopped mid sentence…

Taking a deep breath and motioning for the girls to stay quiet, Paradise was on damage control. "Pops, first of all, to be polite I want to introduce you to my friends Mary and Margaret." There were handshakes all around and tight smiles from the girls, although their eyes never left Paradise. "As for Morning Glory and Dawn," Paradise continued, "the girls were not guilty. Curtis and his men caught the shooter. The girls had absolutely nothing to do with what went on at Frenchy's in Digby." She didn't connect the dots for Pops but she didn't have to. Paradise could tell Pops knew Mary and Margaret had been Morning Glory and Dawn on another day. And it was clear he felt badly.

Thinking hard, all Pops could say was, "Nice to meet you, girls, and sorry about that, Paradise. I was after bein' sure the guys down on the dock knew what they was talkin' about. That'll learn me." Pops turned to leave but not before touching Paradise's arm. "I made a mess of that. I hope you'll forgive me but I won't blame you if you don't." Head bowed he walked away.

Deciding Pops needed to reflect on what he had said, Paradise let him leave without acknowledging his apology.

"Girls, let's get out of here."

Mary and Margaret silently followed Paradise to her car. "What's your pleasure for the rest of your day in my town?"

"No offence, Paradise, but if we go back to your place we'll end up watching that beat- up rabbit-eared ten-inch black and white television you have so I'm all for going for a drive. Is that okay?"

"Great idea, Margaret. Let's head up the line from here and take in the sights. Some beautiful fishing boats are built in these parts. Any interest in seeing a few in progress?"

"Ah, no," followed by a second, "no." Clear enough thought Paradise.

"What about shopping? Any clothes stores around here? Good ones?"

"Frenchy's, here we come. It's another used clothing store, girls, but I promise you it's not at all like the one you were near-naked in in Digby. I know you'll like it, and I'll buy you each an item of clothing," Paradise smiled and stepped on the gas. The old tank was working just fine today.

As they pulled away from the Cafe Central parking lot Paradise felt a need to address the elephant in the car. "Mary and Margaret, I'm sorry Pops made those comments. That was not an Oscar worthy moment. You must be upset. Want to talk about it?"

"Oh, Paradise, we knew when we decided against being pickpockets in favour of trying to become dancers that we would hear things like this. We're used to it, to be honest. It hurts but we've heard it all before. Starting with our own father. You wouldn't believe some of the names *he* calls us."

"Margaret's right, Paradise. No need to feel you've got to work up some sorry for us.

"Today is a good day. You called us your *friends* back there and that sounded real nice to both of us. Let's not talk about bad stuff for now."

They were saved by an oldies song. 'A White Sport Coat and a Pink Carnation' had been released in the mid-fifties and years later three young women belted out every word.

A good day was getting better.

24

Almost a week later, Pops left word at the coffee shop. He wanted to see her. He knew Paradise would be alone now that her two new-best-friends had returned to Toronto or wherever they were from. He still had some unanswered questions about those two girls and wanted to be sure Paradise hadn't been taken in by either of them.

The main thing on his mind this morning though was the personal story he had to continue sharing with Paradise. He couldn't hold the story surrounding her birth and the first three years of her life in his heart much longer. She needed to know. There was so much more. And, there was so much sad.

Pops thought he might ask Paradise to drive them up the line to Bridgetown. He loved the little shipbuilding community in the Annapolis Valley and, more important, he was comfortable there. He might be able to share some of what she still needed to hear while they were driving. He wasn't sure he could look her in the eye but maybe being in the car would make it easier for both of them. Not as personal as it should be, given the nature of the story he was about to tell, but it was the best he could think of for now. At the very least it would help him get started.

The minute Paradise stopped the car, Pops got in and they drove down Cape St Mary Road. Turned left and were on the highway before Paradise spoke. "Got your message, Pops. What's up?"

"I know you have questions only I can answer so should I start talkin' right away? I think we should finish as much of this history lesson as we can today because I am after thinkin' this is wearin' heavy on both of us. Am I right?"

"Roger that, Pops. Talk away. I'm ready. My mother died and you arrived when I was just hours old. Then what?"

She sure does like to get to the point, Pops thought. *Just like her mother.*

Drawing a deep breath and squaring his tired shoulders, Pops felt as ready as he would ever be to relive the worst possible real-life nightmare. He was emotional and specific when he began to share his story. Paradise could almost imagine herself there – in the moment.

Pops remembered every detail and had rehearsed how he would say every word. It was almost a speech.

Paradise didn't interrupt for a very long time.

25

"The day we met you, Paradise, and you know that was about twenty-five years ago, we both changed. We didn't only become father and great-grandfather. Cole grew up and I grew old.

"We knew nothin' about babies or how to care for 'em. We didn't even know your mother had been collectin' clothes for you. One day when you were a few days old and we had been makin' do with rags, Madeline's friend, Elise, came by and showed us the cabinet full of freshly washed baby things that she had been after buyin' from Frenchy's. In another cabinet out back we found about two hundred diapers for you. All made from the softest fabric Elise could find on a tight budget. Your mother sure did want you little one, and she sure did get things ready for your birth too.

"Before I forget, I want to tell you that we had a real nice funeral service for your mother. One of these days I'll take you to where our Madeline is buried. We can even get one of those headstones if you like. But for today I need to concentrate on tellin' you all about you.

"At first our days and nights were crazy. Really crazy.

"We didn't fish. Hell, we didn't even get down to the dock. I don't remember how much time passed before we had to cook even one meal because folks from all over came with food enough to feed an army. Everyone loved your mother and by God everyone loved you before they even laid eyes on you.

"Me an' Cole didn't have any schedule worked out but we took turns doin' things and guessin' what you needed. Basically we fed you, we changed your clothes and we made sure your sleeps were comfortable. We slept when you did, or we tried to. I could sleep anywhere anytime but not my Cole. He seemed to be awake day and night after you came along. He fell in love with you, Paradise, the moment he looked into your cryin' eyes.

"After three weeks or so we agreed that one of us needed to get fishin' or we wouldn't have any money to buy food when the neighbours stopped deliverin' meals to our door. We hadn't earned a penny since you came along.

"Well, wouldn't you know it, before I was due to head out fishin', leavin' Cole home with you, he came into the house proud as punch with somethin' he had put together all on his own. He made it for you. A contraption that would allow you to safely come on board and fish with us. I couldn't believe my eyes. I loved it.

"We had us a real live fisherwoman and you weren't yet a month old.

"Before you came along, Paradise, we really never did worry about any safety stuff – we were goin' out to sea to earn an honest livin' is all. "You either come home or you don't," we always said when anyone asked if we carried worry with us when we headed out to sea. There's no room for worry in a fisherman's lunch box.

"All of that changed the first time we dressed you before headin' to the pier to go to work. Seemed we packed as much worry as we did diapers and food. We loaded you into your 'sea-seat', as your daddy called it, and off we went.

"As we walked down the pier to our boat, every fisherman we passed begged us to turn right around and take you back home. They all offered to share their day's quota with us so we could keep you safe and dry and on land. It was kind of nice, you know, but it also pissed Cole and me off. Did they think we hadn't thought about your safety? We were family for Christ sake. Family looks after family.

"Once they saw how dead serious we were about keepin' you safe at sea they backed off a bit. They all stood around and watched with their mouths hangin' open as Cole strapped your sea-seat into place. Cole came up with your own safe place on board and we were ready to see how you took to bein' a fisherwoman."

Paradise held her hand up. They had returned to the Cape. The car was in park. She was upset.

"Stop, Pops. Stop." Paradise was hurting to the core. She loved hearing the story and was aching to hear more but some of the blanks were still blanks.

139

"Where is Cole? *Where is my father?*" Between sobs and tears Paradise went on. "Pops, I know you're trying to shield me from something but *my God* why isn't my own father here to help you tell me everything? Where. Is. My. Father?"

Pops took a deep breath. "Okay. Okay, sit tight. I guess it's time. We can always get back to the funny stories surroundin' your first day at sea another time."

Pops wrapped his arms around Paradise and whispered in her ear. "I am about to break your heart, my darlin' girl, but know mine is breakin' too."

26

"For damn near three years you fished with us, Paradise. Sunny days. Rainy days. Snow days. It didn't matter.

"If Cole and I went to sea, you did too. And by God you loved every day of workin' with a couple of fishermen.

"Cole didn't love it so much to be honest. He didn't want to think of you havin' a future that started and ended in Cape St Mary. Almost every day Cole would say, 'This is not going to be your future, my darlin' daughter.'

"Before your first birthday Cole finally shared his plan with me – if you could call it that. I called it a disaster waitin' to happen but couldn't talk sense into my boy. He wanted to give you up for adoption. Give you away to some strangers who would know nothin' about you, for Christ sake.

"We were the ones who knew what you liked and what you didn't like. We knew what made you happy and what made you sad. We knew what each cry and whimper meant. Only me and Cole had learned all of these things. Givin' you away, and that would surely be what we'd do if some stranger came to town and took you away – we'd be after givin' you away. Cole's plan was wrong. All wrong.

"Adoption is for kids who don't have parents – you still had me and you still had Cole. Givin' you up was the only thing we fought about. And we damn near came to blows over it. This discussion would come and go and with each passin' day between Cole bringin' it up again I would pray he'd come to his senses and that would be the end of it.

"Today I wish to good God Almighty I had done more than pray about it. I don't care what they say, prayers are not always the answer.

"The day before your third birthday Cole wanted to take the day off and spend it with you on land rather than at sea. I suggested we wait one more day and take your actual birthday off but he wouldn't have any part of that notion.

"The day was a bright sunny one and we dolled you up and took you all the way to Yarmouth for breakfast. You loved your food and en route you sang your own little tunes thinkin' about your meal.

"As we were finishin' up our special meal a couple I'd never seen before, and a third person I'd later learn was from some big-city adoption agency, approached our table. After smilin' sweetly at you, they turned to Cole and one of 'em said, 'Nice to see you again, Cole. Are we ready?'

"My mind went into defence mode. 'Are we ready for what, Cole? What in hell is goin' on here?' I grabbed

142

Cole and shook him, thinkin' I could shake some sense into him I guess.

"Cole nodded his head and introduced you to the 'nice lady'. He hugged you real tight and just like that – you were gone. I didn't have time to blink or ask any more questions. You were rushed away. I would later learn that a fourth person was in the car, at the ready so to speak, to drive you away with your new parents. I cried like I had never cried before. Cole had even more tears than I did.

"I will forever regret what I said and what I did next. Paradise, I hit Cole square across the face. And, I yelled at him too. 'I wish you was dead Cole d'Entremont. Do you hear me? I wish you was dead.'

"Cole hung his head. 'I wish I was dead too, Pops.'

"We drove back to Cape St Mary in silence. Silence except for us both crying. Two grown men crying out loud. I'd never seen that before. It might have been the first time I've ever truly cried.

"It wouldn't be the last. The hurt still wasn't done with me."

27

"We told no one you were gone Paradise. We stayed home. We watched the wasted days go by. We could hardly breathe. Coffee brewed on the stove and guilt brewed in Cole's heart. I could see it eatin' at him. All the time.

"Every mornin' came way too early for two grown men who still hadn't spoken a word to each other. Every night we cried ourselves to sleep all the while wantin' to talk about it. Life can be so unfair and unbelievably heartbreakin'. And two stubborn men living together... well I just wish we had talked to each other sooner than we did. We stayed quiet for too long.

"We were alive but not livin', Paradise. Our life was a total fog. We were missin' you and we were missin' each other.

"Finally, when we knew we needed to earn money or we wouldn't be able to pay our bills we returned to work. Our hearts were not in it but nothin' we could do. Everyone here has to work for a livin'. That's true even now. Back then I think it might have been worse.

"We got out of bed at our normal time. We ate breakfast in silence – I could see Cole wanted to talk. He

didn't though and I didn't either. Dear God in Heaven, why didn't I ask if there was somethin' he wanted to say or get off his chest before we went out to sea? We made lunch, walked down to the pier and boarded our boat. The cries of 'Where's Paradise?' from the fishermen on every boat around us almost killed me right on the spot. It was worse for my Cole.

"There's no easy way to tell you this, Paradise, so I'll just spit it out right here and now. As soon as we were out at sea Cole came to me offerin' the biggest bear-hug known to man. He spoke in a whisper. 'I did what I thought was best for my daughter, Pops. I know her mother would have wanted it that way. I owed that much to both of my girls. Forgive me, Pops – please. In God's name forgive me.'

"What happened next happened in slow motion. I had no idea it was comin'. My beloved Cole turned around and ran to the side of the boat. He looked back at me with tears in his eyes and said again, 'I love her, Pops. I love you too. Maybe she'll come to you one day and if she does you make sure she knows I gave her up for adoption because I love her. I want a better life for my Paradise than I could give her here. What I am about to do, I guess, is because I'm a coward.'

"I have relived this a million times and I swear to you, Paradise, in an instant I saw hesitation in Cole's eyes. He changed his mind. If his plan was to jump overboard he changed his mind. He was <u>not</u> going to

jump. As Cole tried to spin around and come back to me he lost his balance. I couldn't reach him in time.

"Paradise, your daddy fell overboard. He didn't jump. He did <u>not</u>. He fell. Cole disappeared immediately as God is my witness. Part of me died right along with him. I can't explain how I got the boat back to shore. I don't remember anythin' after Cole fell that day. I wish it had been me. I became a very old man in an instant.

"My boat that you see me sittin' on hasn't been out to sea since that day. I never leave the dock. Everyone knows why. I can't do it. I can't – knowin' my Cole is out there. He's out there still.

"Maybe I should've seen somethin' in him that might have prevented his death. Paradise, I didn't know your daddy was any more sad than me. People talk about depression now but I didn't know what that was. I only knew what sad was."

Paradise was in shock as she whispered, "Pops, please get out of my car. I need to be alone."

Pops leaned over, kissed her tear-stained cheek and left her. He watched Paradise slowly drive away and didn't take his eyes off the road until he saw her car stop at her apartment.

Not for the first time, Pops wondered if he had done the right thing. "I sure do hope I didn't frighten you away Paradise." He didn't know how she would deal with so much sad.

28

Bless me, Father, for I have sinned.

I bailed. On everyone.

I left Cape St Mary. I left my jobs. I left my apartment the day before my rent was due. I did this knowing how hard it is for my landlady to make ends meet even with rent money from all of her tenants.

My heart has been smashed to smithereens. *My mother is dead. My father is dead.*

Or... are my mother and father in Toronto? Maybe I lobbed them off too soon. When I learned I was adopted I had a thirst to find my *real* parents. I've dreamed of the day I would look into my mother's eyes and see a mirror reflection of myself. I wanted to know them. To love them. To have them love me back. Now I'm beginning to wonder what makes a parent a *real* parent? Funny that thought didn't cross my mind years ago. During my years in the convent when I had so much quiet time in my cell I didn't once consider this. For a woman who is almost twenty-six years old I seem to be a bit of a flake in matters of the heart.

I sit in row 23. That's my lucky number and I could use a bit of help from Lady Luck right about now. I hope

I have a firm hold of my emotions before this plane lands in Toronto.

I called them just seconds after leaving Pops. I didn't tell them why I needed to fly to Toronto on the first possible flight. I couldn't tell them I was running. I couldn't tell them anything because when I left Pops I didn't know who I was, where I was, or what I would do next.

I call them *them*. I'm a mess.

Poor Pops. He was only doing what I had insisted he do. *Tell me everything and tell me now.* I repeated those words over and over until he gave in.

Our airline hostess is a short and solid woman. She has eagle eyes, a masculine jaw and an attitude suggesting she takes no prisoners. And, she gave me my first drink. *First drink ever.* Seeing my tears and probably hearing my sobs she didn't ask if I would like something to drink, but simply leaned my way saying, "It's a double scotch, darlin' and it works for me every time. Take it. Drink it – all of it." I did as instructed. Soon I was floating and I don't mean because I was in a plane.

I don't know how long I slept. I'm wide-awake now – head high, shoulders back and confidence *kind-of* in tow. To keep busy I'm going to work on my new to-do list. Top ten in no particular order.

1. Figure out what to call *them*.

2. Find the old journal in my bedroom. I know I left it there.

3. Visit Thomas's family.

4. Find Clint – the Ontario-based PI. Ask for help finding Wilmot.

5. Find Marie – Wilmot's partner.

6. Look up Mary and Margaret Ville.

7. Ask my Toronto mother to help me with some personal stuff.

8. Determine if my Toronto parents know Elise.

9. Do they know Alphonse (Pops)?

10. Their version of events on the actual day of my adoption? How did they find me?

"Ladies and gentlemen, please fasten your seat belts. We're beginning our descent..." *What?* I slept through most of a two-plus-hour flight. I must make a note that a double scotch is a great sleeping pill.

I didn't fly alone. Regret, guilt and sadness will follow me off the airplane. The bricks on my back feel all too real. Will Pops be okay? Have I left the Cape for good? More questions than answers.

I'm not even sure what my own name is. I left Toronto as Paradise d Rhodes and return as Paradise d'Entremont Rhodes. Or, am I Paradise d'Entremont without the Rhodes? As Pops would say, "I'm some sad about things."

I was the last passenger on board before I could make myself stand up and leave the plane. I didn't travel with any checked luggage so my exit will be a fast one.

Did they both come? If only one shows up, I hope it will be her because he doesn't understand me, unless we talk about guns of course. I don't have much time left to make a decision regarding what I'm supposed to call them. I can avoid it for an hour or two but at some point I will need to decide if Mom and Dad are appropriate expressions to use.

Will I break their hearts if I *don't* call them Mom and Dad?

***

In a secluded corner of the city, not far from where Paradise's plane touched down in Toronto, a young woman continued the hard work of remembering.

Marie woke up anxious to be out of bed and ready when Mary Rose came to collect her for physiotherapy. She was now able to look after her personal needs first thing in the morning and her nurses continued to praise her for improvements both physical and mental. Mary Rose was working hard with Marie to try to make her 'first thing in the morning' a bit *earlier* in the morning. She still needed lots of sleep and often she slept through half of her day.

Marie worked hard to clear her foggy mind. Her memory banks were not yet in order. She did remember her partner, Wilmot, and the apartment they shared in Toronto. Wilmot had not come to see her yet and Marie assumed it was because he was unable to get to her. She hoped he was okay.

Wilmot had taken Marie to meet his family and she was trying to remember who they were. Did he have siblings?

29

I see Mom and Dad immediately. (That answers my first question – they *are* Mom and Dad.) We hug as if it's our first hug ever – first Mom and then Dad. Dad has never been one to hug at all so this display of affection brought a tear to my eye. Once again, our silence speaks volumes. In this moment it all feels like home – at least for now. I realize it's too soon to be certain.

"We've loved your letters, Paradise, but it's so great to actually *see* you." My mother spoke for both of them. "Your phone call was a bit of a worry though. Are you home to stay, dear? Did something bad happen?" Mom held my hand as we walked through terminal three at the Toronto International airport. We walked very quickly – heads down. She seemed happy but confused and eager all at the same time. Wait a minute, did Mom call me *dear*? That's a first.

My father started the car the second he slid behind the wheel. We were on the highway before Mom and I had a chance to catch our breath. Dad always spoke his mind more freely when we were in the car so I was sure if he had anything to say he'd speak up as we made our way home. I was right.

"Well, did you get your answers, Paradise? Did you find your father?" The way Dad said the word *father* made me realize he'd been hurt by my need to find my birth parents. Thinking back, I probably used the term *real parents* without realizing how it might make them feel.

Clearly there had been no contact with my birth father in Cape St Mary following the day I was adopted. That's how it worked back then I guess. I'm not ready to tell them my birth father is dead or how he died. I need to plan how I'm going to tell them all I've learned from Pops. Is it possible they didn't know my mother died in childbirth?

My head is a mess and my heart is in even worse shape.

The drive home was familiar – Highway 427 South to the Gardner and up Yonge Street to our home at Yonge and Bloor. It took almost as long to drive home from the airport as it took to fly from Halifax to Toronto.

I didn't know how to begin *any* conversation once we were home. Mom asked if I was tired after my flight and I used that as my excuse to be alone. "Would you mind if I go straight to bed?"

I need my room, my bed, my music and my space. My safe space.

I'll figure this out.

30

I slept well my first night back under my parents' roof. It's a good thing too because today I have to deal with some heavy stuff.

Never in my lifetime have I had an image look back at me that looked anything like me. As a child I tried to see a reflection of myself in one of my parent's faces but – *nothing*. Only the mirror itself looks back with the same eyes, the same lips and the same expression.

During my five years in the convent I longed to find my *real* mother and father… to learn whether or not I looked like them. I'll never know.

I moved to Cape St Mary to find my parents only to learn they're both gone. Not even a photograph. The reality of it churns in the cogs of my mind. My parents died so young. They were both younger than I am today.

As I lie in bed I believe I have a bit more clarity about what I need to do. Not to mention the fact that I'll need to bury my overused expression of 'real parents'. I'll do that immediately. The parents on the other side of my bedroom wall are the only parents I will ever have. Warts and all.

I'm going to make this work. It's not all bad – I can tick the first two things off my list. I know what to call *them* and I have found my journal. I still love making lists.

I'm unsure whether I will jump right in this morning and ask my parents how they came to adopt me or if I should ask about my brother first. Surely they have some information about Wilmot's disappearance.

I know one thing for certain. If I stay locked in my bedroom with my journal as my only companion, I won't get any answers at all.

So, enough of this. Time to *man-up,* as the guys like to say.

31

Walking down the hallway Paradise could smell her mother's coffee. She could also hear the angry words coming from her father. Both were familiar.

Ben and Nancy Rhodes had drained the coffee pot waiting for their daughter to join them for breakfast. Paradise must still be sleeping – or writing in that journal again, her mother thought.

Nancy was nervous not knowing what to say to her daughter this morning. She was certain there were many things to discuss.

For Ben it wasn't as difficult. "She either wants to be here or she doesn't. I don't much care one-way or the other. Maybe she came home to hit us up for money. Well, she isn't getting a dime from me. Not a dime."

"When did you ever give so much as a dime to your daughter, Ben?"

Angry Street – that's where my husband chooses to live. Nancy felt sorry for Ben but there was only so much she could do to help his mood today or any day. "Ben, lower your voice," Nancy whispered. "Paradise might hear you. What kind of a start to her day would that be?"

"I don't give a damn."

"Good morning, Dad. You don't give a damn about what?" asked Paradise, although she'd heard every word. She refused to let him ruin her day before it started. He seemed much more angry than she remembered and certainly more argumentative. Poor Mom.

"Oh, it's nothing. You mother's in a snit trying to figure out what you're doing here and what you want from us." Paradise waited to see if her mother would defend herself but as usual she did not.

Paradise spoke *for* her mother. "Dad, I have to say this. I grew up listening to you speak *for* Mom and just before I left this house I finally realized when you quoted Mom you weren't really quoting her at all. You were trying to feed me your own negative thoughts while pretending they belonged to Mom. Isn't that just about right, Dad?"

Where did that come from?

This was the first time Paradise had stood up to her father. The shocker, though, was to see him back down immediately. "You don't know what it's been like for me losing my job and watching your mother go out to work so we could have food on the table. You just don't know what it's like for a man to have to ask a woman for a bit of change. It's different for a man."

Excuses. Excuses. Excuses.

"Tell me, Dad, how is it different? Why would it be any different than how a woman must feel having to ask a man for money? I listened to Mom ask you – beg actually – not for a lot of money but just a bit of *change* over the years. I could *see* how it made her feel. So come on Dad, help me understand the difference."

Nancy's face grew pale. Paradise had developed her backbone while she was away. That would be a good thing, although it would definitely cause more friction between father and daughter. Feeling proud of her daughter's courage, Nancy said, matter-of-factly, "Let's eat, you two. I don't want you fighting right off the bat. Can't you get along for one single day?" Making it a bit more personal Nancy looked at Ben and then at Paradise before she continued. "Please, do it for me if not for yourselves."

Nancy had Paradise's full attention. "You're right, Mom. And I'll do anything for you. I didn't come home for money or in need of anything that you aren't willing to give or share with me. To be honest, it's mostly answers I need. But for now I agree – let's eat."

Over French toast, bacon, fruit and wonderfully brewed coffee Paradise delicately tabled the first of her tough questions.

"Mom, Dad, can you help me understand how you came to adopt me? *Me* in particular?

What did the whole process look like? How did you find me in Cape St Mary, Nova Scotia, when you were living here in Toronto? The two places are worlds apart."

"Let's do this now, Ben. Right now. I've just about had it with secrets." Paradise watched her mother take charge of the conversation. "I'll begin and you can take over if I forget something. How does that sound?"

"Whatever," came the one-word reply from her dad. "Who needs to know stuff from the past anyway? Never did understand how your mind works, Paradise. Makes no sense to me."

There were times when Paradise thought she actually did hate this man. On the other hand, a friend in Cape St Mary had convinced her that *hating only hurts the hater.* It made sense. Plus, how could a former nun hate anyone? At moments like this Paradise's education at the hands of those in the convent seemed a million years ago.

As her mother shared details of how she came to be adopted, Paradise tried to mentally file the information in some sense of order. Following Wilmot's birth Ben and Nancy learned there would be no more children. They wanted Wilmot to have a sibling so they immediately began the adoption process. When Wilmot was still a baby himself they were informed by their adoption agency that a young man in Cape St Mary, Nova Scotia, had a daughter he wanted someone to adopt. They had asked about the mother but no information was made available. The young man's name was Cole d'Entremont and Paradise was his daughter.

As her mother spoke her name a tear trickled down her cheek. Paradise crossed the room to sit beside her. They held hands and wiped their tears away. It was one of many tender moments Paradise would journal at day's end along with the facts she was finally learning.

Ben and Nancy couldn't remember the names of the people from the adoption agency. They remembered the important ones – Cole, his grandfather, Alphonse and Madeline's best friend whose name was Elise. Paradise was stunned to hear the mention of Elise and was anxious to learn of her role in all of this. However, she allowed her mother to tell the story in her own way, and at her own pace.

The first trip to Cape St Mary had been a disaster. "Elise arrived late, with you, Paradise, and she also brought the sad news that Cole wasn't sure he could do this. My first thought was that it was cruel to introduce you to us and then be told we wouldn't be able to adopt you. Your father and I fell in love with you immediately. You were about a year old then. We were heartbroken returning to Toronto without you, dear.

"Adoption rules seemed vague or at the very least different than they are today. Elise was representing your father and that was that – he had decided to keep you so end of story. Your mother was not mentioned but we did learn Cole was nervous about telling his grandfather that he wanted you to be adopted. He hadn't even spoken with Pops about it yet – Elsie confided she wasn't sure he ever would. We asked to speak with your mother but our question was met with a blank stare from Elise. It appeared the file would be closed. "I couldn't get the image of your little face out of my mind," whispered Nancy as she paused to catch her breath.

Softly, with words that seemed to surprise even himself Ben interrupted with, "I couldn't either, Paradise. *I couldn't either.*"

"Almost two years passed with many calls to the adoption agency. No other baby would do. It had to be you or no one. Then the best day of our lives – the call we were waiting and praying for finally came. *'Cole d'Entremont has changed his mind. He wants you to adopt Paradise.'* Again we asked if you mother was aware – no answer in return. It seemed your father would be our contact and he was acting alone." Nancy looked at me and I know she was silently asking about my birth mother. This was not the moment for me to interrupt. She understood and went on.

"The whole thing had to be kept secret from Cole's grandfather. Alphonse knew Cole had once considered letting someone adopt you and apparently nearly lost his mind. He thought Cole had changed his mind for good and understood you belonged with them. As a result, Alphonse wouldn't be given the facts until the moment it happened.

"We would be waiting at a specific place in Yarmouth. Elise would be our driver in case Alphonse caused problems. She knew the area because it was her home. She had practised our swift departure. In a way I felt we were stealing you and Elsie's comments didn't make me feel any better."

With obvious pain in her voice my mother went on. "This time Elise picked us up at the Halifax airport herself and stayed with us the entire time. Cole said he would lie to his grandfather if need be to get you to the restaurant that day – the day before your third birthday.

161

Cole's plan was that your actual birthday would be in our home. The date of your birth would mark the beginning of your new life.

"Paradise, when we saw you walk into that restaurant hand in hand with your father and Pops, as everyone called him that day, our hearts dropped. You looked so happy we couldn't imagine taking you away from the only home you had known for the first three years of your life."

I smiled when I learned my birth father had forced me to wear a dress. And, clearly I was not happy about it. Mom said she could quote me and would never forget my exact words that day.

"'I'm a fisherwoman, Daddy. I wear my fishing clothes like you and Pops. I *do not* like dresses, Daddy. Let's go home and catch some fish. We can eat at home can't we, Pops?' You had no idea what was about to happen. You just wanted to go home and get that dress off.

"Your father finally spoke up. The exchange was swift, Paradise. Your father was crying and your grandfather didn't appear to understand what was happening. We took you from Cole's arms and ran to the car. Elise had the motor running. Honest to God we ran with you in our arms. I know it doesn't make sense to say this, Paradise, but it felt wrong and it felt right."

"To be honest, we thought we'd hear from your father but we never did," Mom offered next. "Hopefully you can answer some questions for us while you're here.

We can understand why Alphonse stayed away. He was so upset I thought he might have a heart attack on the spot. We both felt real sorry for him. But surely your father must have at least been curious, Paradise?"

"I'll tell you all about my father – my birth father – I promise, but can I do that another time? I don't have the heart to relive the facts just yet." Paradise was speaking in a whisper. Wanting to help her, both parents were eager to change the subject. Clearly there was a whole other story surrounding Cole.

Next, after all these years, my mother addressed the letter *d*. "We didn't want to take your last name away from you, Paradise, so we decided to use the letter *d in lower case* as your middle name and would one day explain your adoption to you."

My parents had shared so much with me and as we emptied the coffee pot for the second time I felt the need to share something in return.

I told them about my mother and how she had died just after I was born. "Dad and Pops were out fishing that day, as they were every day. My mother went into labour after they left very early in the morning. She was alone – no phone – no way to contact anyone. Mom brought me into the world as she lay dying. She managed to write a note to introduce her daughter. *Her name is Paradise.* Those are the four words she wrote and pinned to my blanket. Pops kept that tiny, blood stained, piece of paper and now I have it." I couldn't go on. This was the first time I had spoken the words out loud since Pops shared them with me. It was killing me and I could see I was not the only one hurting. I excused myself and went to my room. We were in this together – there was so much to be shared on both sides.

As the water poured over me in the shower an hour later I mentally reviewed my list and crossed off a few more things. As it turns out my parents had met Elise. They had met Pops too. With the few details she had, Mom helped me understand how the adoption agency worked back then, I knew how they came to *pick me* and I knew all about the lower case letter d.

I was getting some of the answers I so desperately needed. I was tempted to take the rest of the day off and wander through the streets of my childhood. In reality I knew that wouldn't happen. Getting answers felt good and I needed more.

32

Number three on my list – number one in my heart. Visit Thomas's family. If I pretend the only reason I'm doing this is because it's on my list, perhaps I won't be quite so anxious.

When I was a kid my dad and I often saw Thomas at the shooting range. If my dad yelled at me, and that happened often, Thomas was close by with a kind word. Dad was always telling me I *stalled* when I took shooting practice. *'There's a difference between stopping and stalling and you're stalling, kid.* Stalling is never good if you *need* to shoot. You stop for a good reason and you stall because, well, maybe because you're a girl. I can't figure you out, Paradise.'

Thomas would often whisper words of encouragement. 'Reload, kid. Don't retreat. Never retreat – especially with your old man. I think he's a bad ass and you deserve better.' One sunny day Thomas really made me laugh when he whispered, 'You're at a firing range for Christ sake, Paradise. Fire a few insults at the guy.' He was leaning so close to me that his long hair touched my face. I loved it. And I loved him too.

Time to reload and fire an insult. From that day on I tried to stand up to my father. At least when we were at the firing range.

I've walked past Thomas's home a dozen times in the last hour. My father told me he moved away. That's all I know. I'm twenty-six years old – Thomas is twenty-nine. Three years older than me so when I last saw him on the eve of my sixteenth birthday he was nineteen. *Yikes. We were young.*

My father could be right about Thomas moving away, but I'm not convinced. He just doesn't like him. He never has. I'm hoping his mother is home alone. I like Mrs Adams and if she tells me Thomas doesn't live here I might cry but I'll believe *her.* I'll find out as much as I can and deal with it later… I guess.

Knock, knock, knockin' on heaven's door. I heard her before I saw her. "Get in here, my darlin' Paradise. Thomas is going to want to know all about you so come on in." His mom was exactly as I remembered her. A country girl, kind of like me, living smack dab in the middle of a very big city. Apparently liking it too because she was still here.

We sat comfortably at the kitchen table I remembered so well. I often came here, as a child trying to get a glimpse of Thomas but never letting on he was the reason for my visit.

Today I had to answer a million questions before I could ask any of my own. And, I had to answer correctly too. When Mrs Adams asked if I was still shooting a gun and I replied with, "Yes I am and loving it," the question came right back but reworded.

"*No,* tell me you are *not* shooting a gun. A beautiful girl like you with a gun? Paradise, what has gotten into you? My dear Lord in heaven have mercy on this child."

As religious as she was so many years ago when Dad first started taking me to the shooting range. Mrs Adams and Mom always said they would say extra prayers for me. The good Lord would *not* like the idea of me having my own gun. *And shooting it too!*

A false laugh from both of us took care of the silence for the few seconds that followed.

My own parents had not yet asked what I'm doing for a living and if indeed I'm still shooting my gun. I was a bit surprised to get the question from Mrs Adams. Maybe because she knew Thomas saw my dad and me at the shooting range so often she was curious to see if I had given it up – now that I have grown up.

A poster outside the rifle range all those years ago said, *'Grow up – Give it up'* and my mother wanted me to take that to heart and put my gun away. The poster related more to gangs from the detail I can remember. The idea behind the poster was to grow up but to *not* join a gang. It had nothing to do with guns, at least that's how my young mind had read the poster. Thinking about it now and the fact that the poster was hanging at the shooting range my mother was most likely correct.

Mrs Adams was never one to mince words. "I suppose you want to know about Thomas, don't you,

Paradise? I called and told him you were home. I asked what he wanted me to tell you if you had any questions. Thomas assured me you would've forgotten all about him long ago. Said I was not to worry."

As if he's forgettable.

I learned so much during my visit. Thomas and his best friend Clint did not stay with the Royal Canadian Mounted Police. Basic training was in Regina and according to Mrs Adams they loved the training but not Regina and certainly not the structure. They both came back home and soon after their return they launched their own little business. PIU – Private Investigators Unstructured. That sounded like Thomas. He loved using words in ways that he could deliver his message without coming right out and saying it. Clearly this message was that he would do things his way and without unnecessary structure getting in the way.

Finally Mrs. Adams got to the detail I was waiting for. Clint is currently running the business from their offices in Port Hope, Ontario. Thomas is very much an active partner in PIU *but* he operates out of another office – *out of town*. The one thing Mrs. Adams would *not* share is where Thomas is living or how I might contact him. *You know, just to say hello.* I wanted her to tell me everything.

The next words she spoke broke my heart.

"Thomas has moved on, dear. He has a family now. You don't need to know the details today and certainly not from me. I gave my son my word that I would not have this discussion with you. It's not my place to say more."

I felt like a fool.

Paradise lost. Again.

33

I left Mrs Adams without saying another word. She kissed my head, gave me a Kleenex and walked me to the door. We were both in tears, albeit I wasn't certain what had made *her* cry.

The silence following her last statement was deafening. I found comfort only when I got to my bedroom and closed the door behind me. This time, even writing my thoughts in my journal isn't helping.

It didn't mean anything.
itdidn'tmeananything.
It Didn't Mean Anything.
It didn't mean anything.
<u>It didn't mean anything.</u>
IT DIDN'T MEAN ANYTHING.

It doesn't matter how you spell it, how you space it or how you say it. It didn't mean anything.

I wish I was dead.

Honestly.

***

My mother left me alone in my room without interruption for a full twenty-four hours. Finally, she knocked on my door and came in without waiting for an invitation. Mom brought with her two cups of coffee, toast with jam and a heart filled with love.

Sitting on my bed, Mom made herself comfortable as she placed the food on my beaten-up old bedside table. Clearly she was here to stay. She handed me a cup of coffee and took a sip of her own.

As if she had to get the words out of her mouth before they burnt her lips, my mother spoke in a whisper. "You've got to help me here, Paradise. Your father has always maintained that Thomas raped you. All these years and you've never talked to me about this. I'm your mother, for God's sake. You were sixteen. Thomas was nineteen. How in God's name could *you* let this happen? I raised you better than that."

Did I actually hear my mother swear? This means she is extremely upset. I need to choose my words carefully. For all these years, my mother has thought Thomas raped me? Good God, where do I begin.

In her first few sentences, and they seemed well rehearsed, it was not lost on me that my mother pointed out I was *only* sixteen and yet she wondered how *I* had let this happen.

There's that 'blame the girl' reaction I have come to hate. So often young women are misunderstood.

I took a sip of coffee. My coffee stood between me and a story that was about to leave my lips for the first time. I had not even written the words in my journal. I had no idea my parents were even aware Thomas and I had been intimate. There are things they still don't know.

34

"Mom, I was *not* raped." I had to get that out immediately. How could my parents think Thomas would abuse me in any way? I knew my father didn't like Thomas but I had no idea his anger was *so* extreme. I was heartbroken to learn my parents had kept these feelings and accusations from me for this many years – a decade. "Thomas did *not* rape me."

In my mind our friendship began on my thirteenth birthday. Thomas and I shared a quiet, almost silent, interest in each other. Admittedly it began at the shooting range but even in the neighbourhood I always knew he was there to help me if anything went wrong at school or at home. I could talk with Thomas about anything.

Well, I could but I couldn't. I was too shy to actually carry on a conversation with Thomas. It was easier for me to insult him in that schoolgirl kind of way. My insults were met with an 'ouch' and then Thomas would duck as if I had hit him. I was always checking to see if Thomas was nearby and I was certain he was doing exactly the same thing. He told me he liked knowing I was around and that I brightened his day. There was definitely a connection.

Trying to explain this to Mom was difficult. One minute I was saying we liked and respected each other and in the next I was telling her I liked him too much to engage in conversation. I can't imagine how Mom's head must have been spinning because mine sure was. I had danced around this long enough.

I took a very deep breath and began. Thomas and I made sure we were alone on the eve of my sixteenth birthday. Without going into the detail of where we were, how it happened and why it happened I did manage to admit to my mother that we had made love. It wasn't rape. It wasn't sex. It was making love. I didn't *let* it happened. I *wanted* it to happen. We wanted each other. I was in love with Thomas and I knew Thomas felt exactly the same way. We were caught up in the emotion of it all. You could argue Thomas should have known better and you could argue he took advantage of me but no – I don't buy that. I knew what was happening and I wanted it as much as he did.

We made love and it was beautiful. Everything about Thomas was beautiful and kind and sexy. The way he looked, of course, but in this case it was the way he behaved with me. He kept asking if I was okay. He must have said, *"Do you want me to stop?"* a million times. I didn't. He didn't.

Mom sat close to me as I poured my heart out to her. She understood. Thank God for that.

I didn't know what Dad *thought* he knew, and I would not be having this conversation with him anytime soon to find out. Mom was okay with that. She listened to my entire and all too personal story without interruption. "Mom, maybe if I had shared this with you on my birthday things would have turned out differently. When I told Thomas I loved him but I had made my decision to be with God he was so angry with me. I wanted to become a nun and Thomas said he *could not and would not* accept that. I felt so alone. I ran away from everything and everyone. I'm so sorry I hurt you and Dad. I know I hurt Wilmot too and I'll tell him how sorry I am the second we find him." *I prayed we would find him soon.*

Mom and I cried as I shared the details of my secret. It was only after hours had passed, the coffee cups were empty and I said, "Now he's gone. He has a family already, Mom. What I thought we shared *didn't mean anything* to him," that she interrupted.

"That's simply not true, Paradise. Now you listen to me, young lady." I suspect Mom used those words to take me back to my youth. I heard that expression many times leading up to my sixteenth birthday.

"I had a sneaky suspicion Thomas was in love with you. I had no idea the strength of that love until your brother came home after taking you to the convent. Paradise, Thomas knocked on our door only minutes after Wilmot returned. Your father opened the door and Thomas stood there in that locked and loaded stance, as you and your dad like to call it. Honestly, he filled the doorway." Mom took a deep breath and went on.

"Thomas had no idea you were gone. His first comment confirmed this. 'Paradise and I want to talk to you – all three of you. Where is she? Honest to God, I'm not moving and I'm not leaving until we sit down together and talk about this – about us. Paradise and me.' Wilmot came to the door and told his friend to go home. Wilmot said something about you being out with friends to celebrate your birthday. I'm sure Thomas knew it was a lie." Mom paused, but not for long.

"Paradise, Thomas knocked on our door every day when he could get past the concierge and if he couldn't do that he would call. And call. And call again. He begged me, when he could get me alone, to tell him where you were and how he could reach you. Honestly, I don't know why I didn't tell him. I wish I had. When he returned to Regina he called us to say he would continue to find a way to track us down every day. 'Every goddamn day,' is apparently how he left it with your father." I could imagine Dad's reaction.

"When a career with the RCMP didn't work out and Thomas came back home, he continued his daily routine of asking if he could talk to you. Paradise, he begged me to tell him how he could reach you. He was determined and he was focussed like no one I had ever seen." When Mom bowed her head I assumed that was the end of her story. I leaned in to offer a hug, but there was more.

What came next was 'Breaking News.'

Mom raised her hands to indicate she was not finished. "Then all of sudden, Paradise, Thomas roared into our home one evening and in one long and confusing sentence he told your father and I to, 'Listen up'. If I remember correctly his exact words were, 'I'm not sure you'll ever see me again. I'm leaving town. I'm leaving the country actually but I want you to know this – the two of you. I will *never ever* set foot inside a Catholic church again. I'm going to make things right for Paradise if it kills me.' Paradise, your father and I didn't understand what Thomas was saying or why he was saying it. He wouldn't elaborate and to be honest he frightened both of us. We didn't see him again. That was the last conversation I had with Thomas I swear on my mother's grave."

There was more news. Mom kept in touch with Thomas's mother – they were lifelong friends. She talked at length about what Mrs Adams' friendship meant to her. Mom described with great clarity the day Mrs Adams told her Thomas had his own business. His first case was huge as he had explained it to her. He was investigating the alleged sale of babies through a link with the Catholic Church. As a faithful supporter of the Catholic Church, Mom did *not* want to hear this. She didn't press Mrs Adams for details. This was so typical of my mother. At any hint of a negative story involving the Catholic Church she would turn away. If the story sounded illegal Mom would have no part of it. Not her church. No way.

Clearly Mom had *not* made the connection between the details shared by Mrs Adams and the comments by

Thomas that he would never step inside the Catholic church again.

Dear Mother of God, what did Thomas find out?

35

When my mother told me Thomas had worked on a case involving newborn babies and the Catholic Church I could hardly breathe.

Did Thomas investigate *my* convent and if so when? *Was I there*? I need to speak with my brother. Wilmot where are you?

As I explained to my dear friend, Sister Mary Elizabeth, over and over, I knew what I was doing. "Yes I did – I do – love Thomas but not as much as I love Him." Sister Mary Elizabeth had loved only Him her entire life so she really couldn't grasp my heartache. She admitted her love for Him freely but still wanted to understand and support my decision to give my daughter up for adoption and to go to such lengths to keep Thomas from finding out he was a father. She sometimes even questioned my commitment to Him but never my love for my daughter. It may have been the right thing to do but the day I said hello *and* goodbye to Hope was the saddest day of my life. There was 'so much sad' as Pops would say.

I remember one extremely sad young girl, Ruth, who had just given birth at the convent and wanted her baby to be adopted too. She was also sixteen. Mother Superior entered the birthing room to speak with me about one of the other young mothers. She saw Ruth crying and approached her. In an unkind tone of voice, as if she was talking to a total stranger rather than a young girl she had seen here every day for the last eight months, Mother Superior said, "Control yourself now. No more tears. Sorry for your loss. We encourage you to leave the convent as soon as you are strong enough to do so. Put this terrible experience behind you and move forward with your life. Be a *good girl*. Let us pray."

What?

I am convinced to this day Mother Superior not only didn't know Ruth's name, she didn't know if Ruth had been told her baby died or was being adopted. Sister Mary Elizabeth and I called MS a *bitch* that night. Then we hurried to the chapel and said the rosary followed by a whole string of prayers.

Following my own 'experience' as it was called, I worked hard on my recovery. Emotionally I tried my best to believe it all happened exactly as I had been told and one day Wilmot would confirm the details for me. Sister Mary Elizabeth and I joked that I didn't have stretch marks and that had to be a good thing. A sixteen-year-old body is pretty resilient. No stretch marks and no baby either. I could pretend to be okay.

I really needed my mother after giving birth. My emotional healing took far more time than my physical healing. However, Mom didn't know I had been pregnant so Sister Mary Elizabeth and I decided, in our youthful minds, that she wouldn't want to help me… because of my 'sin'.

My 'At Seventeen'came and went. I *did not* learn the truth at seventeen. I wouldn't learn the truth for a very long time. I was unsure what had happened to any of the other babies born at the convent, but I had to believe my little girl lived and was now in the hands of parents who loved her. I silently spoke with her every day. *My Hope.*

I thought a lot about Thomas during the dark days after I gave my baby away. *Our baby.* He would never know what I had been through. Would he even care? If he cared in the first place, why didn't he find me and get me out of there before I gave birth? Looking back I placed much of my negative energy on Thomas's broad shoulders. His shoulders were much broader than mine. He could handle it.

Today, I need to find my brother. If I could talk with Wilmot some of this might make more sense. I have no idea if he stumbled upon what was happening at the convent but I suspect not. Sister Adeline would have simply placed a call to him telling him Hope had been born and the details of her adoption.

36

An early morning walk down Yonge Street would clear my head. Hopefully…

Mom used to tell Wilmot and me that a walk *up* Yonge Street was very different from a walk *down* Yonge Street. She said we would discover this for ourselves over time. Through the fog both inside my head and in front of me (Or was that Toronto smog?) I understood what Mom was saying. And, it seemed to be true even today. I found myself in the midst of parts of Yonge Street that had not *cleaned up*, so to speak. Strip joints were everywhere.

Of course the strip joints made me think of Mary and Margaret – their Morning Glory and Dawn days behind them. Before they left Cape St Mary the girls talked about the horrible life they felt I saved them from. They knew stripping and even prostitution was where they were headed if they didn't turn their lives around. Surrounded by men constantly talking about the *big money* awaiting them, the girls (both minors) had lost focus on the difference between right and wrong. Respect and no respect. Mary and Margaret thanked me a million times when I dropped them off at the Halifax International airport for their return to Toronto. They promised to write and give me their address. So far, no letter had arrived.

The girls were on my list of people to locate, but this morning, it was all about clearing my own head.

Yesterday had been a heavy day for me. I needed a long walk before facing the goals on my list this morning. On the other side of Yonge Street a poster caught my eye. I crossed the street thinking *oh-no-oh-no-oh-no*. Almost life-size posters outside one of the more well known strip joints. Morning Glory and Dawn. I recognized the girls immediately. I did *not* recognize the huge breasts they were proudly displaying. Those breasts had *not* come to Cape St Mary. Oh my God, what have these girls been up to? Did they not learn from anything I said?

The hour was early but the doors were open so I marched in – my first step *ever* inside a strip joint. *Colour me nervous.* I was instantly angry and needed some answers. The joke, it seemed, was on me.

I met the sleazy manager who was happy to inform me that indeed Morning Glory and Dawn were still in the business. They were the headliners this week and why didn't I come back and see them in action as he put it. He kept touching my shoulder as he spoke. He made my skin crawl. I learned the pictures for the posters had been taken only five days earlier. Patrons forked over *top dollar* to meet *his* girls and have them sign their poster. This was one proud manager.

I did some fast calculating. Mary and Margaret *might* still be underage. With all that I had on my mind, and on my plate, at the moment I couldn't deal with this. I couldn't ignore it either. I would give this one to Clint and was certain PIU could have a field day with it. I had enough background information on the girls to put Clint on the fast track to getting them out of this lifestyle – new breasts and all.

Not wanting to tip anyone off, when the manager asked if I wanted to leave a message for *his* girls (again his words, not mine) my reply was all lies. "No, that's okay. I guess I've made a mistake. Morning Glory and Dawn, as you call them, are clearly not the women I'm looking for. Good luck, sir, with your star attractions." I nearly gagged on my own words.

His chest puffed out as he winked and held the door open for me to leave. "Think about coming back, sweetheart, I'll give you an autographed poster at no cost and I'll buy you as many drinks as that fine body of yours can handle. Come any time. Just ask for Big Daddy." *Sure, that'll happen.*

I will *never* understand men. Except for Thomas of course and that brings me right back to reality and everything I learned yesterday. I may not have understood Thomas at all. How can that be? I can't let him cloud my every moment right now. I have things to do and people to see.

I'll pass my Morning Glory and Dawn file on to Clint before I head back *home* to Cape St Mary.

Somewhere between going to sleep last night and my walk this morning I have made a decision. Cape St Mary will eventually be my permanent *home*.

37

I need something serious to focus on this morning.
Something important to my family and to me – my
brother Wilmot. Mom and Dad and I have been
pretending Wilmot is not on our minds. I know that isn't
true for any of us.

Breakfast became a very heated affair.

"Mom, Dad, I came home with a list of things I want
to delve into while I'm here. Right up there on my list is
Wilmot. What went wrong with my brother? What
happened? How did he get mixed up with bad people?
Do you have *any* information we can start with? And, I'm
sure the *most* important question for all of us, *where is
he?* Let's work together on this and find the answers we
need." As I spoke, I was looking at Mom and watching
Dad out of the corner of my eye.

Instantly my father flew into a rage. This was a rage
I'd never seen before. Worse than when he lost his job.
Worse than when Mom found a job and even worse than
his rage over Thomas and me.

"If you're going to talk about *that brother of yours*
you can get the hell out of my house, Paradise. Wilmot
does *not* exist. He walked out on us without a word. Not

even to your mother and that almost killed her. I'll never forgive him for that, do you understand me?" When Dad said, '*Do you understand me?*' he flipped the kitchen table over and stood literally in my face. Our noses were touching. Clearly when it came to discussing his son, Dad needed to intimidate.

"Intimidation won't work with me, Dad, so you can drop that tactic. If you can't talk to me and be totally honest, I'll find someone who will. Mom, how about you? Can you fill me in?"

I regretted my words immediately. I watched Mom drop her shoulders, and her tiny body seemed to shrink before my eyes. She tried her best to speak. "Well, dear, your father has forbidden mention of Wilmot in this house so I really can't help you."

I picked up on three of Mom's words – *in this house* – and replied with, "I need some fresh air, Mom. Let's take a walk."

We could hear Dad screaming as we waited for the elevator. "Don't you spend one minute talking about him. Wilmot is *not* my son." Hitting me one more time with his words Dad went on, "Paradise, don't you dare upset your mother, do you hear me? *Do. You. Hear. Me?*"

I thought about how sad Dad's words must have made my mother. Clearly he felt the loss of his son as much as Mom did but attempted to hide his feeling behind hers. If he was hoping we wouldn't see how devastated he really was it wasn't working – not at all.

I took Mom's hand as we exited the condo to begin what would be another very long conversation.

***

How do kids become bad kids? I'm not sure that's a question that can be easily answered by anyone.

During a lengthy discussion my mom shared that Dad developed an absolute hatred for Wilmot when he couldn't get answers about his son's job. He had met a couple of the men Wilmot worked with. Dad referred to them as players. These were men who could show Wilmot big money, fast cars and all the women he could handle. What my parents knew for sure was that Wilmot had money and was driving a flashy car. He wouldn't tell them where he worked or what he did with his time. With the exception of his girlfriend, Marie, Wilmot's friends *never* came to our apartment. He was staying out all night and this in particular was making Dad a very angry man. He felt ignored and embarrassed by his only son. Mom cried when she said, "Paradise, Ben feels any man who doesn't respect his father isn't a man."

Mom tried to dry her tears as she went on. "I even worried about Wilmot when he was right in front of me. Among other things, I didn't like the way he was treating Marie. I didn't know much about her but she deserved respect, certainly from her boyfriend. He called her *the wife* even though they weren't married. I really didn't approve of the expression. When I tried to challenge him on this he yelled at me, Paradise. Honestly, he said some awful things. 'Get with the times, *Mother*. You've been listening to stupid for too long. Don't let Dad make you stupid too. We all call our women *the wife*. Meat started it and we like it. It's a tradition now and it's funny so get over it. End of story.' If your father had heard that particular rant I'm certain he would have killed your brother with his own hands."

Wilmot said so many terrible things that day, Mom couldn't remember everything. The words she could remember were burnt into her mind and into her heart.

This is not the brother I remember.

Because Wilmot gave money to Mom every time he got paid, Dad was left feeling his own son was throwing in his face the fact that he couldn't support his wife. I cried as I watched my mother hang her head. Moments passed before she was able to go on.

"One day your father called Marie a whore, Paradise, and I didn't have the backbone to stand up to him and speak for Marie. I didn't argue with Ben in support of Wilmot's girlfriend and I sometimes feel that my actions, or lack of actions, cost me my son. I know it isn't really true dear, but I got so depressed after that. There were dark days when I felt I had lost you and then I watched my son slip away from me. I was lost. Paradise, one day I actually went to church and prayed for God to take me so I may be by His side and understand all of this – or at least some of this. If I couldn't be with my children I wanted to be with my God."

189

Mom would rather be dead than with my father. That didn't say much for Dad. I hadn't understood the depth of Mom's sadness until now.

There were so many things I could say to my mother but to what end? I see it all the time in every job I have – women being abused at the hands of the man they love. At the coffee shop I listened to a man tell his wife she was fat because she always ordered chocolate (and by the way, she was not even the slightest bit overweight). At Frenchy's a man tore a pair of jeans out of his wife's hands, telling her she would look like a fool in those pants and even when I am cleaning someone's house there is a man throwing insults.

In discussions about this very topic, women have often opened up to me. Their views are very different from mine. 'I have nothing to complain about. My husband has *never* hit me. It's just that his words are mean and sometimes I let it get me down. He doesn't mean what he says when he yells at me. When he gets really mad, he says it's my fault because I provoke him and I guess maybe there are days when I do.'

That makes it okay?

I truly want to help my mother. Dad – not so much. He doesn't want to change and he certainly won't listen to a woman. He doesn't feel he needs anyone's help. Everyone is wrong but him. Honestly, I hate to admit it but there are days when I can't be bothered. I can use my time more wisely. In the back of my mind though, I know this is such a negative attitude for me to carry around all the time.

Perhaps one day, Dad and I will work to resolve what our true feelings are for each other – and why. I could begin by taking some of the advice I give to others now that I think about it. There was a time when Dad and I shared special moments and I want those moments back.

Mom sat for long stretches of time in silence as if trying to spit her words out. I had great respect for the quality of quiet from all those days in my cell at the convent, so staying still wasn't a problem. I could wait all day. I didn't want to assume the conversation was over and tried to take my lead from my mother.

When it finally seemed Mom had nothing more to say, I let my mind wander.

What now?

I have to pick a day, soon, to see Clint about Morning Glory and Dawn. First though, I'll talk with him about Wilmot. I'll make sure my brother gets some uninterrupted time. He deserves it.

I took Mom's hand in mine as we walked home. Our relationship had changed. Not only were we mother and daughter – I had the feeling we were friends. We were good friends who had just crossed that bridge that allows you to talk about *anything and everything*.

38

I had blisters on my blisters when Mom and I got back to the apartment last evening. Mom on the other hand wore sensible shoes so her feet were fine. I'm learning my mother is sensible about most things. Dad met us with a downturned face and a look that suggested he was not to be spoken too. This would not be a problem. It was a quiet supper and an equally quiet evening.

As I reflected on Mom's earlier input I understood Mom and Dad really hadn't learned any of the details surrounding Wilmot's disappearance. Whatever happened to my brother remains a mystery. My parents have no knowledge of Marie either and that bothers me. Is anyone looking for Marie? *I will.* I want to find them both. At the very least perhaps they're together.

Hopefully, with Clint's help I'll be able to get the answers my parents and I so desperately need.

I still have plenty of work to do but I've accomplished a lot since arriving back in Toronto not that long ago. I'm pleased with my progress. In fact, my list is almost complete. Time for a new one.

1.   Locate Clint and ask for his help finding Wilmot *and* Marie. If we find one, we might find the other.

2. Share with Clint what I know, or think I know, surrounding circumstances under which babies were leaving the convent while I was there. *Hopefully everything was legal.*

3. Of lesser importance, speak with Clint about Morning Glory and Dawn. I say *lesser* only because Wilmot and Marie are far more important at the moment. At some point I might have to take the girls off my list. Not yet though.

Note to Self – You do *not* know Clint. You have never met Clint and you have no idea if he'll be willing or able to help. I'm making a note of this because I'm putting all of my eggs in one basket. I should give some thought to a plan B. (Currently there is *no* plan B.)

4. Develop a timeline for returning to Cape St Mary.

5. Make arrangements for Mom to visit. Ask her if she would like to go to Hawaii on vacation with me one day. A trip to Hawaii would be my dream vacation.

6. Find Elise once I'm home.

7. Spend quality time with Pops. I owe him. I demanded the truth and he told me everything leaving nothing out.

8. Find a way to have a *career* rather than multiple jobs. I want to have *one* focus – private investigator. Pd PI. That means giving up my three current jobs without leaving anyone in the lurch. I'll continue to eat at Cafe Central but won't be on staff. I'll purchase my clothes at Frenchy's but will no longer be a part-time employee. Finally, the only house I'll clean will be my own. *No*

longer will I work for those who have looked down on me even though I willingly helped them by cleaning their homes every day if they asked. They will need to hire a new cleaning lady.

Cleaning lady – that's how Mrs Canso introduced me to her friend when they came to the coffee shop for lunch. Without even mentioning my name, she turned from me to her luncheon companion and said, "Good Lord, *this* is my cleaning lady." Lowering her voice to a whisper she went on. "What kind of people do they hire in this coffee shop?"

Perhaps when I am no longer cleaning her house, I'll tell Mrs Canso that behind her back my friends and I called her Mrs Can't-so with the implication being *I can't – so you have to do everything for me*. We called her a bitch too but I won't share that. I sometimes remind myself I was once a nun after all!

9. Purchase a new wardrobe. I'm going to ask Mom to help me select some new clothes while I'm in Toronto. I could use a pair of jeans that actually fit, a few jackets with a bit of colour and maybe we could hunt down my first pair of high-heeled shoes. *Killer high-heeled shoes.*

10. Book an appointment with a hairdresser. My first professional haircut is high on my to-do list yet I rank it #10 – because just writing it down makes me nervous. I'm far more nervous about having my hair cut and styled than I've ever been about shooting my gun.

11.   Spend time with my Dad. I'll do this more as a favour to my mother. Not sure anything will be accomplished but I'*ll* try.

As always, my list is in no particular order and by no means complete. It's also one of my more rambling lists. My goodness, since I was eleven years old I have found comfort in journaling. Clearly, today is no different.

Bless me, Father, for I have sinned. Bitch is a word I need to remove from my vocabulary.

Learning as I go.

39

The sky was cloudless and the hour was early. Out of bed and enjoying the view from my bedroom window, I could already feel the heat from the early morning sun. Time to make some decisions. My mind was racing. This would be a double-whammy day.

I was certain my parents could hear me moving around and would soon follow the smells of breakfast – bacon and eggs happening in the kitchen. *Everybody up.*

"This is a lovely surprise, dear. If I don't make breakfast in this house it doesn't happen." I knew Mom meant it as a compliment rather than a slag towards Dad.

"Dad, I scrambled the eggs the way you like them and Mom, the bacon is crisp just for you. We even have fried tomatoes for a bit of colour. This is how I serve my customers at Cafe Central. How does my presentation look?"

Nothing could get me down this morning so I ignored my father. "Waste of a tomato at this time of the morning. I'm not even hungry but I guess I might as well eat since I paid for the groceries."

I waited until our plates were empty (and yes, the tomatoes had been eaten too) and I'd poured second cups of coffee before I asked the question.

"Mom, do you know a good hairdresser downtown? It's time for me to get a proper hair cut and it might as well be today. I need it styled and a treatment too, as you can see." With nothing more than a grunt Dad left the table and the room. No thank you from him but that was par for the course.

"Paradise, I'm sure you'll need an appointment so you may not be able to have your hair cut today but what a delightful idea. May I come along?"

I knew Mom and a neighbour took pride in cutting each other's hair, so I appreciated this not being thrown out as an option. "Oh, make no mistake, Mom, *you have to come*. I might faint merely walking into the salon. I've never been, as you probably know, and I'm actually nervous. Where do we start?"

With a warm hug Mom said, "I'll be right back, dear. You wash those dishes up and get them in the drainer for now. We have things to do."

"Okay, but believe it or not there's one more thing I would like to do today, Mom. I'm in the mood to try on high-heeled shoes." I was talking to the back of her head. What was my mother up to?

Before I finished washing the dishes I heard Mom make a phone call from the other room. "Hello? Yes, I would like to make an appointment for my daughter to have her hair cut. I think she'll need a treatment too."

There was a short pause followed by, "Today, this afternoon, if at all possible," and then, "We'll be there. Thank you so much."

Who are you and what have you done with my mother? Mom looked both happy and confident as she came back into the kitchen. Confidence was not something Mom had an abundance of. In her hands were two white envelopes with my name clearly printed on both. I took the envelopes from her trembling hand and began to open one. "No no, open the other one first."

Inside the envelope I found a $100.00 gift certificate for Vidal Sassoon Hair Salon on Yorkville Avenue. $100.00 would pay my rent in Cape St Mary! I was speechless.

Mom was crying but through her tears she offered the kindest, most gentle and caring message I had ever received. "Paradise, I didn't have the opportunity to help you get all dolled up for your high school prom. By the time you were thirteen I was already saving money for your hairdo not knowing you would be gone before graduation. So when you called to say you were coming home I went right to the hairdressers and bought this gift certificate. I really want you to have it. It's *my* gift to you, dear. I know I'm at least a decade late but I hope you'll accept it."

I cried realizing how much Mom had actually been hurting while I was in the convent. I was wrong to have judged her in any way.

"Mom, I'm sure I can get my hair cut in Mavillette for under $20.00." I didn't know what else to say.

"You're not in Mavillette now, dear. I can't get my money back so you're stuck with it. And by the way, your appointment is for three p.m. this afternoon. Now open the other envelope. What's inside will tell you where we will begin our day once we get organized and ready to head out."

Mom turned to leave the room but still had more to say. She wasn't ready for me to open the envelope just yet. "Actually, Paradise, let's get dressed first. Then you can open the envelope and we'll take off."

***

Speechless – once again. I couldn't believe my eyes. The second envelope contained *another* gift certificate for $100.00. This one – The Bay. I knew there was a Bay store near us so we would be shopping within minutes. Mom explained this gift was for new clothes and because she was sure we would need *more* than $100.00 she had a bit of extra cash in her pocket as well.

We walked to The Bay and went straight to ladies' clothing. Mom understood jeans would be my top priority so that's where we were headed. The jeans were *so* soft to the touch, each pair on a hanger rather than in bins as I was used to at Frenchy's *and* they had a million different designs to chose from. The prices *did not* impress me. I could purchase jeans at Frenchy's for under

$3.00 a pair. Mom was quick to suggest I forget all about used-clothing stores for now. All the designers I sorted at Frenchy's were here as well: Louis Vuitton, Armani, Ralph Lauren, Chanel and more. Not easy for me to forget the alternative pricing when shopping from racks versus bins. Eventually, we did manage to find racks with non-celebrity labels. Still, nothing was cheap.

With the assistance of more than a few sales clerks, Mom steered me through the dizzying process of buying everything I needed. She helped me choose the most flattering colours and styles, offering advice on what to pay full price for and what to search out on sale. The only thing that stumped us both was my size. We shared a very long laugh at my expense. Only the sales clerk knew for sure.

On to lunch. As we chatted and digested our morning's events, I thought back to when I was a young girl dancing with my mother. Today felt like that. We had danced our way through The Bay.

Looking across the table at my mother's smiling face, I felt my love for her grow and as the talk turned to Wilmot I loved her even more. I had not been home at the time and didn't fully understand how profoundly my brother's disappearance had affected both of my parents. We spoke about Wilmot and our childhood days together in what had been a happy home. I promised Mom I would find Wilmot. *Dear God, let this be a promise I can keep.*

With lunch finished, it was time for our visit with my new best friend – my hairdresser.

40

Metal furniture, mirrored walls and the smell of money in the air. This must be where the wealthy come to have their hair done by their favourite hairdresser. I've heard about it but never *lived* it up close and personal.

Before we could close the door behind us Mom and I faced a barrage of questions. "Can I take your coat?" *Not wearing one.* "Can I bring you coffee?" *Not here for coffee.* "Who is looking after you today?" *I don't know but I want to turn around and run out the door.* Then came the magic words. "Where did you buy that beautiful red top?" Was she talking to me? No one has ever *ever* asked where I purchased anything.

Maybe this Vidal Sassoon Hair Salon idea wasn't so bad after all. It just took more than a few seconds to get used to all the *swank.*

Once again my mother took charge. "Paradise has an appointment for a treatment and haircut." Pointing to me and under her breath she added, "We have a gift certificate for $100.00. It's important to me that this be a very special experience for my daughter. She has *never* had her hair cut professionally."

I cringed when I heard, "What do you mean she has *never* had her hair cut? You don't mean *ever*, do you?" I wanted to run as fast as I could. Thankfully, a very professional hairdresser who stepped up, stepped in and took over, saved me.

"Paradise, what a beautiful name. My name is Frankie and I'll be looking after you today. Come with me.

"Would you like your mother to come along too? Sounds like this is a very special day for both of you." In that moment I would have followed Frankie anywhere.

Not one word mentioned about the condition or length of my hair, (it was so long I could sit on it) or that I was shaking from head to toe. How would he manage to cut my hair with the state I was in? Frankie figured it out.

Pulling up a stool he spoke directly to me. It was as if no one else was in the room, or the salon for that matter.

"Paradise, this is a very special day for me too. I'm humbled that you trust me with your first haircut. Tell me a little bit about yourself. For example, do you wear a hat at work? Do you work inside or outside or a combination of both? Are you comfortable using a blow dryer or curling iron?"

Like he didn't already know the answer to his last question. "How long or how short do you want your hair to be when you leave me today?" Sensing he had hit me with too many questions he tried again. "Just sit back and tell me about yourself."

"I live in Cape St Mary, Nova Scotia, very near the ocean. It's often damp or raining which means my hair can get wet during the day. My mother lives here in Yorkville. I work as a private investigator and before you ask – yes, I do carry a gun."

"Not today I hope?"

"Not today." I knew he was trying to make me smile. I tried.

"Uniform?"

"No, my own clothes," I replied proudly, looking at my new red top and fabulous new jeans.

"And can I assume you're not used to taking much time to style your hair in the morning?" This was said with another big smile and his hand on my arm.

"Your assumption is correct. I think I would like my hair long enough to pull back in a ponytail for work but short enough so when I want to wear it down it has some style. Does that make sense?"

"Absolutely. Now let's get started. First, some coffee, ladies, or maybe something a bit stronger to fit the occasion? It's five o'clock somewhere so not to worry."

My mother replied instantly, "I'm game if you are, Paradise. Do you have brandy here?"

Frankie laughed and spread his arms wide. "No, but we do have some very nice wine if you promise not to flaunt it. I don't offer a drink to all of my customers." Even if he was lying I loved the gesture.

Frankie's workstation was about the same size as my apartment. No kidding. He drew his comb through my hair again and again until there were no tangles (which took a very long time.) "Let's do this in two stages. I don't want to cut your hair too short. While it's true hair always grows back, it's also true that your first haircut *must* be special." The first snip of the scissors made me jump – literally. "Ah, this is where the wine comes in. Take a sip."

Two hours flew by. Cut to several inches below my shoulders and treated with the best-smelling-whatever-that-was treatment Frankie rinsed my hair one final time. Before my eyes he created a new me. I liked what I saw in the mirror as he dried my hair. This was a first. *Honest to God.* I rarely looked in the mirror.

I wasn't sure how much credit we had left from our $100.00 gift card but I soon found out. When we added in our tip for Frankie we had *zero* credit left. How is that even possible?

As we were packing up to leave, Frankie gave me a fist full of samples. He loaded my purse with samples of shampoo, wash-in-conditioner, leave-in-conditioner and styling gel. When I asked his advice about purchasing a good hairdryer Frankie lowered his voice and said, "We sell the hairdryer I used on your hair today, Paradise, but go to the Bay. They have the same hairdryer. You don't need to pay these prices." Great guy.

As we walked home arm in arm, with my hair blowing in the breeze rather than weighed down by the length of it all, I thanked Mom one more time.

"My pleasure, dear. I hope we can have a day like this again while you're home. I know you won't be here forever."

"We have lots of time, Mom. Plus, I still have to find those high-heel shoes, remember? And I need you to help me with make-up choices too. After all, I can't leave Toronto dressed to the nines with my sneakers on and a makeup-free face.

One of the very best days of my life just happened and it happened with my mother. I entered the elevator at the condo feeling blessed.

Tired, lovely and blessed.

41

The rant was non-stop. Meat was spinning out of control. No one could make him stop shouting long enough to listen to anything they might be able to offer. Nothing ever changed with Meat. He had to be in control and he was always mad at someone. On this particular day, Meat was mad at everyone.

"*She's here?* You're telling me Paradise is here? *In Toronto*? Not in some fancy apartment on the Upper West Side of Manhattan after she gave up her *look-at-me-I'm-a-nun* attitude?"

You could almost see the smoke rising from Meat's ears as he continued yelling. "We travel to some crappy town in Nova Scotia looking for the *oh-so-special* Paradise and all the time she was in Toronto and literally right under my nose? Are you *all* that stupid? How could you *not* know this?"

He wouldn't listen. Meat's rant didn't allow anyone the chance to share details of how they had very carefully followed Paradise from the convent to downtown Toronto to Cape St Mary, Nova Scotia, and now back to Toronto at her parents' home. The only voice he could hear was his own.

"Most of you were here the night Wilmot came in and proudly told me he was quitting his job. Remember guys? Wilmot thought *he* could make the decision to take off with his precious little whore. You saw what I did to him with my own hands did you not? If no one here wants the same treatment you'll tell me where Paradise is and you'll tell me right now." Meat walked the length of the warehouse and looked every man in the eye. He was making sure they knew he was serious.

"If anyone is in touch with Wilmot it will be Paradise. She has always been his *precious* little sister. How he has stayed hidden from me for this long angers me to the point I could kill someone – someone *else* I guess I should say." Meat laughed at his joke. No one else was laughing. Not funny.

"The only reason I let Wilmot walk out of the warehouse that night was because I thought he'd be dead before he reached his car. There was not a bone in his body I hadn't broken as far as I could tell. You'll remember how many times Wilmot fell as he staggered to the exit. Somehow he kept getting up and taking one more step. I still thought he was a dead man. Come on, you must remember we called him a dead man walking don't you?" No one spoke.

"At the very least I expected Wilmot would drop dead when he reached home and saw the little surprise I arranged for him there. While I was beating his ass, Marie was receiving the same treatment in the comfort of her own home. She thought she could quit and send that little bit of information to me via her slag of a husband? I only wish I could have been in two places at the same time."

A couple of things had gone wrong for Meat that terrible evening. Wilmot lived and so did Marie. Meat knew an ambulance had taken Marie to the hospital. He lost track of her but didn't much care because he was certain, *absolutely certain*, his man would have left her braindead. She was useless to him and she hadn't been much of a secretary either in his opinion. And the only opinion that counts is Meat's.

The fact that Wilmot not only lived but managed to disappear and stay off the grid to this very day was the cause of Meat's rant.

"Wilmot owes me at least one more baby and, the truth is, he owes me a lot more than that. The police shut my business down and I know he had something to do with it. *I just know it.* He won't let anything happen to Paradise so we find her and he comes out of hiding. Easy as that guys. Have I spelled it out clearly enough for you?" He let it sink in.

"Bring Paradise to me." Again, no one spoke.

42

The Toronto sun is bright to the eye and cold to the flesh as it rises in the sky in front of me. I'm chasing the sun eastward as I drive out of the city just after five a.m. in an attempt to beat at least some of Toronto's hectic morning rush-hour traffic. That, plus the fact I was up all too early in anticipation of today's events.

I'm wearing my *whodunit* hat and as Pops would say, 'I'm after gettin' answers' before I put this day to bed. It might be a long one and I'm ready for whatever might come my way. I've waited and wanted this for a very long time. If necessary this day will stretch into tomorrow and beyond. I need my brother. Today is about Wilmot.

Several days ago Dad surprised me by suggesting I take his baby on the road to find the PIU offices. He was certain they had an active file on Wilmot and was hopeful they had uncovered something. "Clint and his partner should be able to help us, Paradise."

Until Dad's last comment I assumed Clint's partner was Thomas. Dad was quick to clear that up. "When Thomas left town, from what I hear, Clint took on a new partner by the name of Jim Taylor." Never heard of him.

Learning Thomas may no longer even be involved with PIU made me sad. In all likelihood I will never catch up with him.

While Mom was having a bath last night Dad brought it up again and this time he was more specific. He also made it more personal. Lowering his voice Dad said, "Paradise, I honestly believe Clint has answers concerning your brother's disappearance. I learned some time back that he was looking into Wilmot's activities. I don't want your mother to know I'm even asking you to get involved with this. She thinks I've come to grips with it but that couldn't be further from the truth. I try not to talk about it with her. Hurts too much. For me and for your mother the hurt is almost unbearable."

I began to speak but stopped when Dad held his hands up. "No more." Several minutes passed and then, "My son is missing. My daughter is a private investigator. *You* find Clint and *you* get some answers about my boy. I need to know. Do this for your mother and for me too. Please." I couldn't recall Dad ever saying please.

The baby he spoke of was his car – his pride and joy. Dad was the owner of a Cadillac Eldorado. The car had not been new to him but new enough and it was a beauty. A tank by my standards – admittedly a beauty all the same. A Cadillac Eldorado Fleetwood Six De Ville.

Sure.

The PIU office is in the small town of Port Hope, a bit more than an hour's drive east of Toronto. Shouldn't be hard to find even with my lousy sense of direction. So here I am on the road. Dad's car is so big I suspect if I speed up a bit it might take off and I could fly to Port Hope. I struggle to look forward while playing with the dials on the radio.

My first companions were Simon and Garfunkel as they sang 'Bridge over Troubled Water'. I could relate. It was the next song I couldn't relate to. 'My Woman, My Woman, My Wife'. Quick, play something else. 'The Most Beautiful Girl' Thanks for nothing, Charlie Rich.

Maybe I should listen to music heading *back* to Toronto rather than this morning when my mind (not to mention my heart) is all over the map.

Beside me in the passenger seat, and protectively wrapped in Mom's trusty long sheet of waxed paper, sits my lunch. My mind reached back to a simpler time.

Growing up, Wilmot and I often made fun of Mom's sandwich wrapping skills as we sat in the lunchroom at school. She always used four or five times the length of waxed paper required. We knew there would be no beginning or end to the strip of waxed paper covering our sandwich. Rather than have our friends make fun of us as we unwrapped our lunch, we made fun of our mother. Today, I would take it all back. Mom was everything to us and often we took her for granted.

Regardless of the wrapping, nothing could ever take away the delightful taste of my Mom's baloney sandwich. Today is no exception. I can't wait until lunchtime and who says lunch had to be at noon? It's now eight a.m. so late enough for me. I can always eat. Anytime, anywhere. White bread, mustard (no butter allowed – Mom's rules), salt and pepper and two pieces of baloney. Gone. Delicious.

When Mom learned I had borrowed Dad's car for reasons not shared with her, she immediately offered to make my lunch for the trip. She didn't ask any questions and that told me she knew exactly where I was going. She didn't need to ask. Mothers are like that and mine is no exception.

What I know for sure is that the PIU office, and hopefully Clint, is just past the Port Hope drive-in. When I called the office a receptionist gave me directions to their front door. She asked for my name but I declined to offer it. I want Clint to have little time to prepare for my arrival. Not sure why I feel that way. I'll deal with those feelings another time.

***

I'm here. In Port Hope. Cars are angle parked. Works for me.

A large and very professional sign on the door confirms I have arrived at my destination. *PIU* in bold brass letters – my heart skips a beat. What if Thomas is here after all? What if he isn't but Clint knows where he is?

Silently I reprimand myself. I'm here to find out what happened to my brother and where he is today, not

212

to find out about the only man I have ever loved. I can't seem to extend my hand to open the door. I silently stand on the porch. I turn around and admire the detail on this beautiful historic building. I wonder if they have the entire first floor. Anything to stall going inside. My nerves have gotten the best of me.

The front door swings open. "Paradise, tell me it ain't so. Is it really you?"

I turn to face the voice.

Rough calculations suggest the man in front of me stands a proud six feet four inches tall. A beautiful package indeed. A chin that has surely been chiselled to give it that killer look, blond hair pulled back into a tidy ponytail, faded jeans tighter than mine, and a not-so-cool baggy lumberjack shirt. If this handsome creature is thinking the shirt hides his beautiful physique I've got news for him. *Wait a minute. Where have these thoughts come from? This is so not like me.*

I still haven't given my name so I try to speak.

Extending a hand to shake mine he suddenly changes his mind and lifts me off my feet in a bear hug to rival all bear hugs. "Thomas is going to be beyond upset that he missed you. Come on inside, Paradise. When Kathy said a woman had called for directions to our office but wouldn't leave her name I suspected it might be you. Word had it you were back in Toronto." Letting me go, he went on, "Just a matter of time before you arrived here I figure."

A second voice from an inner office joined the conversation. "This big bear isn't much for manners, Paradise. He isn't bothering you, is he? I'm Jim by the way and you may have guessed Clint is the man guilty of nearly assaulting you."

I didn't hear a single thing Jim said. I was stuck on the words, '... *upset that he missed you.*'

Is Thomas here? I decide not to ask, not yet anyway. "Come on in, Paradise, where are my manners? Kathy is out but the coffee is hot and you have our undivided attention. What brings you here?"

"Not that you need a reason," offered Jim.

If the PI business is slow these two could be male models. Maybe they are. No photos on the desks. Nothing of a personal nature visible at all. I can't make any assumptions so I will leave it at two *easy-on-the-eyes* PIs.

Honest to God, I can't think straight. My mind is racing and my heart is beating so fast they can probably hear it. I'm glad I made the decision to wear my new clothes. At least I can feel good about how I look even if I have not yet opened my mouth. In the moment, I'm thinking I look slim and every bit as good as the men in front of me. In the convent Sister Mary Elizabeth used to say,'"When I'm feeling fat I think about food but I *do not* eat it and sure enough – slimmer by supper.' She always made me laugh with her comment. Thinking of Sister helped me to relax a bit.

Squaring my shoulders and putting on my tougher, smarter, meaner face I turned and looked Clint directly in the eye. "It's about Wilmot. I need to know what happened to my brother. I need to find out where he is and who's responsible for his disappearance. Can you help me, Clint? Yes or no? I promised my parents when I left Toronto early this morning that I would return with answers, even if they come in bits and pieces."

Silence all around for a rather long and uncomfortable moment.

"Give us a minute will you, Paradise? We need to clear our schedule for a bit and can do that by making a few phone calls. Will you be okay here if we go to our other office?" Without waiting for a reply they left and that was fine with me.

Clint seemed eager to help and I was already beginning to feel more comfortable around him. And, honestly, it's not hard being around Jim either. I am about to spend the day with two very handsome men.

What in God's name is happening to me and to my thinking process? Maybe this is an example of how the female hormones work. Bad timing for mine to *finally* show up. I have bigger fish to fry.

43

"She's here. It's her. *Paradise is here.*" Clint was talking to no one in particular. "It was only a matter of time. I told him that a million times. Damn you, Thomas. This should not be up to me."

Turning to Jim he continued. "When we go back in there, take your lead from me. Whatever you do, *do not* talk about Thomas. I can't stress this enough. Do not even mention his name."

Clint and Jim had moved to their inner office and closed the door. In actual fact, there were no clients booked for the day. Jim was beginning to understand what was going on. The lady on the other side of the office was *her*. The woman he heard Clint and Thomas talking about every time Thomas was on the other end of the line. *Every time.* It was always hush-hush and until now Jim had not given it a whole lot of thought. What kind of a puzzle was this? Other than a rather interesting one. Lots of time to put the pieces together Jim figured.

Jim knew when to ask questions and when to stay out of it. Clint and Thomas had considerable history, including RCMP training and leaving the force at the same time. Their early RCMP departure was followed closely by setting up this PI business. They opened the business with two on the payroll. Clint had given him work when he needed it. That was enough to earn Jim's loyalty and silence as required. Who was he to ask questions? Yet, he had to ask.

"Clint, tell me more. Does this woman's brother have anything to do with one of our main cases?"

Jim couldn't stop with the questions. "Talk to me, Clint, you owe me that much. What's going on here?" He could hardly catch his breath. He wanted to ask a few personal questions about Paradise too but this was not the time.

Paradise was one beautiful woman. They were both thinking the same thing. Jim would bet on it.

"I need to think. Shut up for a second." Clint drained his coffee cup and slowly poured a refill, giving him time before he continued. *He had to think.*

Thomas and Clint always knew Paradise would come back one day and when she did she would be looking for answers. Especially given that her brother is still missing. She would focus on Wilmot before bringing out her list of questions about Thomas. Clint could only hope that would be the case. Why should everything fall on his shoulders when it was Thomas who held all the cards. *How far should I go if she asks about Thomas? How much do I say? And, God help me, does she know where Hope lives?*

Talk about love being blind. Clint was one hundred percent certain that Paradise, and only Paradise, owned

Thomas's heart yet she knew nothing about it. *About any of it*. How was it even possible that she would *not* know?

Clint had first met Thomas at RCMP boot camp and they became fast friends. The very day Paradise was driven to the convent Thomas began his quest to find out what had happened to her. He had been home in Toronto on leave for a long weekend when she disappeared. His search for Paradise continued to weigh heavy on his mind when he returned to Regina. Thomas could not understand why she had left home a mere twelve hours after he last saw her. He felt certain something was *off*. His love for Paradise was the first thing he shared with Clint the day they met. She was all he could talk about when they had down time.

Clint was certain of one thing. Thomas was obsessed with the girl. At the time she was exactly that. A girl.

Today – not so much. The girl is all grown up.

44

Paradise used the quiet time to collect her thoughts.

There were muffled voices coming through the wall. It didn't sound as if anyone was actually on the phone cancelling appointments as had been suggested. Clint and Jim were talking with each other – no one else. That was okay. After all, Paradise didn't actually arrive with an appointment on the books, so let them have a moment to gather their thoughts and get their story straight. Paradise had all day long.

Clint and Jim re-entered the room wearing different expressions. This look was not personal. It was professional. Paradise spoke first. "You're all about business I see. That's great. Same goes for me."

As Clint spoke Paradise could see the photo Jim was holding. She didn't recognize the face. "His name is Meat Cove, Paradise. He is actually from Meat Cove, Nova Scotia. Believe it or not he legally changed his name to Meat Cove some years ago." She recognized the name. Wilmot had told her and her parents about his new boss. He was so excited to be working for the man he called Meat.

Clint continued, "His name is the least of our concerns at this point. Meat is or was Wilmot's boss. Additionally, Marie is or was Meat's secretary *and* Wilmot's girlfriend. Marie's location is presently unknown although we did have a lead on her for a while when she was in the hospital. Wilmot disappeared the very night Marie was beaten and left for dead. We believe it was Wilmot who called for an ambulance before disappearing. Paradise, do you know anything about either Meat or Marie? I know it's a long shot."

"Yes," Paradise replied in a whisper. She didn't have the strength to speak any louder. "I know the name. Wilmot worked for Meat. That's why he quit school before graduation. Because he was making so much money doing God knows what. I have never met Meat but I do know Marie. Wilmot brought her to our house a few times. I liked Marie and have wanted to speak with her. The policeman I spoke with in Toronto suggested she might be dead. Do you think that's possible?" Paradise didn't have a chance to continue.

"Hold on. You're telling us you *know* Marie? What the hell is going on here?" Clint immediately apologized for his language. "Christ on a stick, I'm sorry for swearing, Paradise, especially with you having been in the convent and all."

In spite of everything Paradise had to smile. "Clint, your apology comes with more swearing in case you didn't notice. And, for your information, I have been out of the convent for some time now. May I continue, gentlemen?"

Paradise related all of the detail she could remember surrounding Marie's visits with her and her parents the few times Wilmot brought her home. "I am convinced Marie didn't know much, if anything, about the business Wilmot was involved in. She told me she was Meat's secretary but added that for the most part she counted cash and made notes as directed. She said Meat didn't like her, or anyone else, questioning him. I believe Marie had the bruises to prove he was hitting her but the one time I asked about a bruise on her cheek she clammed up and said nothing else through that entire evening." Thinking further, Paradise added, "Marie did ask that I not tell Wilmot I saw the bruises. She said she always tried to keep the discolouration covered because she knew if Wilmot saw any bruises on her at all he would either kill Meat or die trying." It had not been lost on Paradise that Marie spoke about multiple bruises. Clearly she had been beaten more than once.

Over the next five hours three PIs wrote details on a flip chart as each fact was shared. They were hoping three heads were better than two.

Paradise remained silent as Clint laid out the facts. "Meat is connected to a well-known drug ring in Toronto with additional connections that reach far outside of Canada, especially into the United States. He appears to be the leader of the pack. We believe Marie was on Team-Meat even before she met Wilmot, and yes, we too have heard she might be dead. We've heard it from numerous sources. Meat is known to kill anyone who crosses him so leaving his gang is not an option for any of his members. That would include both Wilmot and Marie of course."

Clint seemed to pick his next words with great care. His look said something along the lines of *I-shouldn't-be-the-one-to-tell-you-this*. "Paradise, there's more. We have confirmed that at the time Wilmot disappeared, Meat's *main* business was not the drug trade. He was buying babies at birth for next to nothing and selling them at a huge profit. The drug trade was just a front. Meat was basically stealing babies from a number of sources but I have to tell you, Paradise, Catholic convents were right up there on the list."

Paradise saw Clint's lips moving but her mind wouldn't comprehend. *Did Wilmot do what he promised when my baby was born? Was he there? Is all of this connected somehow? And what about Wilmot's other promise – to never tell Thomas. Did he keep his promise?*

"Paradise, I'm sorry if this is hard to hear? Are you okay?"

"Did I mention I'm a private investigator, gentlemen? Forget the fact that I'm Wilmot's family for now and tell me everything you know. Please don't leave anything out. It would appear I've been living in the dark for far too long."

Well into the night the decision was made to call it a day. Paradise was given what appeared to be Jim's apartment above the business and the men retired to Clint's quarters across the hall.

They owned the building as it turned out and living on site helped to pay down the mortgage. *Smart as well as handsome.*

45

Clint couldn't wait to bring Thomas up to date. He was sure Thomas would have considerable input of his own in terms of next steps. Would the circumstances be enough for Thomas to jump on a plane? That was the sixty-four million dollar question. Clint wasn't prepared to make that phone call just yet.

Morning came early and with lots of hot coffee in hand the work continued.

"Paradise, let's review a few things," began Clint. "The fact the two main people we're investigating in the disappearance of your brother have been in some form of contact with *you* is a major concern. Marie has met you on more than one occasion and Wilmot would have spoken about you when they were alone so she would be able to tell Meat a fair bit about you. We also have to assume, for your own safety, that Meat has heard about you directly from Wilmot as well – *proud of my sister* sort of conversation when they were sitting around. He would know all he needs to know about you. If Meat thinks you can lead him to either Wilmot or Marie – *you are in danger.*"

Clint was pacing back and forth as he spoke. "When you arrived here yesterday we focused on Wilmot's disappearance and Marie to some extent as well. We have to consider a very significant twist in this story. Paradise, *you* may have become front and center in this case whether we like it or not."

"We'll figure this out, Paradise," Jim jumped in. "We'll do it together. You've got us in your corner. And Thomas too." He added the last part because Paradise was as white as a ghost.

Paradise gave the PIs her best smile and closed her eyes for a minute. She promised her father some answers and she was going to get them. "Just give me a minute, will you please? I desperately need to collect my thoughts and review what I've learned so far. Would you mind if I go for a walk?" *By myself.*

"Not a problem, Paradise. Jim and I have a few things we need to sort out and errands to run as well. Do you want that walk or would you rather stay here and relax for a bit while we're out?" Paradise replied without a word... by stretching out on the most comfortable chair in the room. The men made a hasty exit.

"We need to leave her alone for a bit, Jim."

Jim's immediate, and not too quiet, reply gave Clint something to consider. "Are you forgetting she's a private investigator? If you're thinking Paradise is a weak woman, you need to get that thought out of your head. She is, I suspect, as strong as we are and maybe stronger."

"I'm thinking no such thing. Give your freakin' head a shake."

If looks could kill...

***

"Where do we start?" Clint kept his voice down as they took the back booth in their local coffee shop. Back to work. Jim looked at his partner. He knew Clint had more to say.

Clint seemed to have aged a decade since the moment Paradise arrived. As he sat down his shoulders slumped, he ran his hands through his hair and said, "Biggest case ever. Let's figure out our next steps."

Over the next two hours, among other things, Clint shared more personal detail surrounding the connection between Thomas and Paradise. He made sure Jim understood, one more time, the importance of never taking the lead with Paradise when talking about Thomas.

Jim tried to understand all of the hidden messages in what was being said. He could hardly believe the story. What a mess. *What a mess.*

Knowing Paradise would be expecting them back about now the PIs reviewed what they knew and what they still needed to know.

1. *Paradise* – how do we protect her?

2. *Thomas* – confirm with him what we do and do not share with Paradise. (Do this behind her back. Doesn't seem quite right.)

3. *Meat Cove* – he's our common thread but is he the reason Wilmot disappeared?

4. *Marie* – is she alive and if so where is she?

The PI's decided to split up.

Jim would talk with Paradise. They needed to understand her short and long-term plans. Had she moved back to Toronto permanently or would she be returning to Cape St Mary? How much time was she prepared to devote to this case?

Clint had the tougher task. He would call Thomas and tell him everything from the moment Paradise walked through their doors. He definitely needed to plan his strategy before making that call. Clint knew one thing for sure. Thomas would either be pissed or pleased.

Clint would also bet money that Thomas would demand to speak with Paradise on the phone – in the moment – after all these years.

Bloody well time.

46

Paradise could reel off her goals without taking a breath.

Jim sat back and drank it all in. He was blown away by what she said and how she looked. "Hands off," he kept hearing in his head.

Paradise had returned to Toronto for a number of reasons; a few were personal and those had already been attended to. "Some of my goals were to take care of myself for a change and I've done that. Trust me, you don't need details," was how she explained it. Jim had no idea what that meant but she sure enough did look like she had been taken care of. He reminded himself to *not* say that out loud.

Paradise spoke of her parents, her birth parents as well as her parents in Toronto. She talked about Pops and Elise back in Cape St Mary and her three jobs that kept her busy day and night. She tried to anticipate Jim's questions before they came. Paradise knew she was giving him more information than he probably needed but she couldn't stop talking. Nerves at work.

"In addition to all of the goals I have mentioned so far, high on my list of *things to do* has been to find Clint and through him hopefully find my brother. Now that I have found Clint, and you too of course, how are we going to find Wilmot? Any ideas?"

Jim continued to sit quietly knowing Paradise wasn't finished. "I do plan to return to Cape St Mary at some point in time. If I'm needed here, I'll be here. I've made friends in my little community and found employment that didn't come easy and I'm definitely going back when our work here is done. And, there is *one* more thing. I want desperately to work full-time as a private investigator and I want to do that in my hometown of Cape St Mary."

Jim started to speak but Paradise interrupted. "To be honest, Jim, and I hate to admit this, I'm totally unnerved to learn that I'm linked to Meat, Marie and God knows who else." Paradise took a breath. "Having said all of that, do I think I am in danger? I don't know. *I just don't know.*"

With the hint of a smile Paradise concluded with, "That's a wrap for me, Jim. Over to you. What were you and Clint planning while I was doing my own thing? When you came back I could hear you, you know. Not in detail but I heard you argue then agree with each other only to argue and then agree time and time again. I'm guessing you drew the short straw and therefore had to be the one to come over to talk with me. Sorry, I know I'm still talking. I'll shut up now."

Jim had yet to contribute to the conversation. Paradise touched his arm and asked the big question.

"What does that leave for Clint to do while we're talking?"

Jim didn't have the answer. Actually that wasn't quite true. He had the answer. It just wasn't his place to share it.

47

It was clear to Jim that Clint had the tougher job. He had to call Thomas.

An empty rum bottle sat at his feet (in fairness it had been opened some time ago so was not completely full when he poured his first drink of the evening.) Clint's hair was rumpled. He had a habit of running both hands through his hair whenever he was frustrated. He was beyond frustrated at the moment. His ponytail was no more and it seemed he was trying to pull his hair out or at the very least hide his face behind a mask of hair. It was not a pretty picture.

Jim could hear only one side of the conversation. It wasn't hard to guess what was being said at the other end of the line. Clint kept trying to interrupt without much success until he raised his voice and wouldn't back down.

"I hear you. *I hear you*, Thomas, but listen to me for one goddamn second will you." Clint stopped and shook his head as if rearranging his thoughts. He walked around for a few seconds and then dove in again. "Here in Port Hope daylight is feeble and I worry that Paradise is tired out. My mind is fried so I can't imagine how she's feeling." Clint continued to pace. "Seriously, Thomas, putting Paradise on the phone at the end of another bitch of a long day is not fair to her. It's not fair to Jim and me either." He lowered his voice. "Think about this. She has not heard your voice in *how many years?* You want to talk to her *now*? I'm not doing it, buddy. *Not doing it.* We can continue this discussion or I can hang up. Which will it be, Thomas? Your call. "

Jim jumped in with both feet. "Put Thomas on the speakerphone. And, let's keep it down. Paradise is one thin wall away. She could hear bits and pieces of you and I speaking earlier, Clint."

"No speakerphones. Pick up on another phone, Jim, and we'll have a three-way conversation without the concern that Paradise might overhear." Clearly Thomas was not going to let this go and he sure as hell was not going to let the conversation end if he could prevent it. He was in charge and it was apparent he was used to having control. Perhaps having his own way too.

Jim briefed the others, sharing everything about his time with Paradise. In turn, they brought him up to speed regarding their discussion about Wilmot's disappearance and his connection to Meat. Thomas was adamant that Paradise was in danger and needed protection. He wanted her to leave town. *Today. Now.*

"Good luck with that," offered Jim. "I just met the woman yesterday and I can tell you she will introduce her '*Sexism in the PI force theory*' faster than you can blink an eye. She has already told me she won't be hiding away while we hunt down and fight the bad guys. Claims she can shoot a gun as good as, if not better, than all of us and by the way she said it I tend to believe her. Lots of confidence in her voice. She is up and ready to work before dawn. We learned that little detail this morning."

"I hear ya," said the voice on the phone. "Paradise was up with the birds even as a kid. Not surprising that she is ready to work by six a.m." Thomas went on to tell them, in a bit of a melancholy voice, how Paradise came to the rifle range with her father at least once a week and could shoot a gun better than any man at the range by the time she was eleven years old.

Jim was beginning to understand just how much history these two had. It was also clear how Thomas felt about Paradise.

48

The ringing of the phone startled Paradise. Her parents' wouldn't be calling her this late in the evening. She wasn't sure they even had the PIU phone number. The only other people who knew she was here were the two men a small apartment away. She wasn't sure why they would call when they could simply knock on the door. It was their apartment after all.

Her inner voice was saying, '*Just answer the phone Paradise.*'

"Hello?"

Silence on the other end of the line followed by, "Aloha, kid. Fired any good insults lately?"

Thomas. *It was Thomas on the phone.* After all these years Paradise was paralyzed at the sound of his voice. So much time had passed. He even remembered their private joke from so many years ago. It was the day at the shooting range when he told her to fire insults at her father.

Not wanting her to hang up on him, Thomas tried another approach. "If I told you I have a .357 Smith &Wesson and a Ruger .44 mag with your name on both, would you come and visit me?" Not much of a pickup

234

line, he thought after the words left his mouth. This was not going as planned. Too bad he dialed the number *before* thinking this through. So far the only thing Paradise had said was hello. He needed more. Thomas waited.

"Aloha. Did you say Aloha?" Paradise had found her voice. "Are you on vacation? Where are you, Thomas?" Her voice was a whisper.

"Paradise, I live in Hawaii. I live in Honolulu to be exact. I work my PIU files from here and am in constant contact with Clint and Jim. We speak almost daily."

Paradise tried to speak but Thomas interrupted her. "My partners are going to be angry with me so we need to talk fast before they barge in.

"How are your Mom and Dad? God, I gave them such a hard time after you left. I was desperate to find you, kid. I still worry about your parents, just as I worry about you.

"I can't begin to tell you how sorry I am about the disappearance of your brother, Paradise. We'll find him. I promise you we'll find him."

This was beginning to feel easier and it was her turn to interrupt.

"Thomas, *what is going on*? Why are you living in Hawaii if you're partners with Clint and Jim here in Port Hope? What do you know about Wilmot's disappearance? Are you honestly working on his case with these two? My parents are going nuts needing answers and quite frankly I am too. Help me understand what is going on please. If begging is what it will take, I'm begging you."

She sounded all grown up and Thomas found himself wondering what she looked like. He had not seen Paradise since the eve of her sixteenth birthday. God knows – if she's half as beautiful now as she was then... he had to stop his mind from wondering. Now was certainly not the time.

"Paradise, listen carefully. I can and I will explain everything but you must *come to me*. I need you to fly to Honolulu. I've checked into flight times and you can fly direct tonight. Your ticket is waiting for you at Toronto International airport. I need you to leave immediately to catch the flight." Thomas waited for his words to sink in. He wasn't expecting the response he got.

"As you proud male PIs like to say, '*Are you fucking nuts*?' Walk away from what I'm doing and fly to Honolulu so you can *explain?* You listen to me, Thomas. I have a life here and I have a life in Cape St Mary, Nova Scotia. My parents are waiting for me in the same apartment building in downtown Toronto that you will remember. Mom and Dad are hopeful this trip to Port Hope will cough up some answers about Wilmot's disappearance. My brother is my *only* focus right now. You want me to walk away from my life and come to you as you put it? *Come to you*? Really, Thomas?"

Paradise thought she would never understand the male mind. Never. *Come to me*. Who was he kidding?

"Well, when you put it that way kid," Thomas said trying to lighten the mood for a moment or two.

"Stop it. I'm not a kid any more, Thomas."

When Paradise remained silent he knew he had to say more. The words Thomas spoke next stopped Paradise in her tracks. "Paradise, I had hoped to say this to you in person. Face to face. I know what happened. I'm sorry you had to deal with all of it without me. I wish you had felt confident enough to turn to me." Thomas took a deep breath and continued. "I know everything because Wilmot called me. Don't be mad at him for breaking his promise to keep your secret. He loves you like crazy and he was only protecting you. I think his call to me was his last conversation with anyone before he disappeared."

Listening carefully, but in shock, Paradise could hardly believe what she was hearing.

Thomas continued. "Come to Hawaii and once I explain everything we'll fly back to Toronto together if that's what you want. I'll do whatever you want. I promise you, Paradise. Please."

"Why? Why are you in Hawaii in the first place, Thomas? Help me understand. Why did you leave Toronto?"

"To protect my family!" Thomas was shouting now. "You're a private investigator so figure it out Paradise. *Figure it out.* Get over here. I'll say it again. Your ticket is at the airport."

With harsh words Thomas hung up and said a silent prayer that she would be on that flight.

Thomas would be waiting at the gate tomorrow morning. He wouldn't be alone. Someone very special was anxious to meet Paradise. Thomas didn't have a plan B. If she didn't show up he'd have to start over and try to explain things in a way that made her desperate to come to him for answers. Paradise was a smart woman. She could fit the pieces together.

This had not been his proudest moment. If only he had thought more carefully before he dialed the number and heard her voice.

Thomas would be disappointed in the morning. Paradise would *not* be on the plane.

49

"*Yes,* we know you want answers, Meat. We're trying to give you answers but you've got to let one of us speak long enough to give you our status report, as you like to call it. We *do* know her every move and today might be the day." *Shut up and listen* is what they really wanted to say but that would be a huge mistake.

"Paradise has gone to Port Hope to meet with some half-ass private investigator. She arrived yesterday and is still there today. We thought she would head back to her parents' place last night but that didn't happen. Her car is still in the parking lot and she's inside so she's shacked up with the guy. What do you want us to do, boss?"

With a killer-calm on his face and his trusty Sig Sauer in hand Meat was ready. Bring 'em on, he thought as he pondered driving to Port Hope himself and blowing the wannabes to kingdom come. He fancied a she-bang kind of day. The *she* being Paradise. He couldn't wait to bring her down.

"I'll be out of the office today, boys. Something I have to take care of. *Someone* I have to take care of." He said with his standard fake laugh.

Meat's boys understood he meant business when his attitude turned this bad. This was one mean son of a bitch even to those who had been loyal to him through every botched drug deal, every botched baby-snatch and every police chase through the underbelly of the city of Toronto. Meat was convinced Paradise knew exactly where Wilmot was hiding and he was determined to make her talk.

It was all about revenge for Meat. He wanted to take his former employee out and would do exactly that. Killing Wilmot in cold blood the second he had some answers would put a smile on his face. His gang had learned over the years, one at a time when they dared to disobey Meat, no one gets away with crossing the boss. None of his men wanted any part of Meat's take down of Paradise and were relieved to hear him say he was going on his own. *Let him go* they thought, but just in case he was testing them, they said it again.

"What do you want from us, boss?"

After some thought Meat said, "Give me confirmation Paradise is with *one guy. One guy only.* Is that one hundred per cent accurate, boys?"

The answer, which would prove to be wrong, came quickly and from more than one of the men. "Just Paradise and the PI as he calls himself. That's it. Two of them in there, boss. No more."

"What I want then is an address and a *solo* road trip to Port Hope. My adventure will end with bullets in the nuts and in the hearts of Paradise and the dick with her.

Let me be, boys. I'll share all the gory details with you when I get back."

Meat took off but not before levelling one more group threat. "Be damn sure you're here when I get back. You know what'll happen if you aren't. And it'll happen to every damn one of you if you're not careful."

Meat had already decided once Paradise led him to Wilmot he'd kill her too.

His reason for killing her? Because he could.

50

Paradise didn't wait for Clint and Jim to *come to her.*

All good-willed out, she barged in to the other room with the words literally falling from her mouth. Paradise couldn't say it all fast enough and decided to dive right in. If they were in agreement with Thomas, she needed to set them straight. And she wanted to do it fast.

"I just spoke with Thomas."

"*What?* You called Thomas in Hawaii? Good God, Paradise, we didn't even know you had contact information for him. What were you thinking?"

"Don't interrupt me, Clint. I *did not* call Thomas. He called me." She took a breath before going on. "Thomas thinks I'm in danger and he wants me to fly to Hawaii. He appears to think I can't protect myself and apparently he feels you guys can't either."

"Are you kidding me?"

"No, I am not kidding you. Thomas wants me to fly to Hawaii *tonight.*"

"Tonight?"

"Shut the hell up, both of you." Paradise surprised herself with her outburst but she had to make them shut up and listen to her. "Don't worry. I'm not going anywhere. *No one* is going to tell me what to do or where to do it. Not Thomas. Not either of you. I make my own decisions."

This girl is pissed thought both Clint and Jim. Not at all what they expected. That must have been one hell of a conversation.

Paradise continued. "I *came here* because I need answers. My parents need answers. You both know that. I suggest we put Thomas on the back burner for now and get to work." She couldn't believe she just said that. "My brother is out there somewhere and I'm confident we…"

They were interrupted as the front windows were blown out of the building. Shots fired. Blood everywhere as the PIs scrambled.

One down.

One bleeding.

One terrified.

***

Meat got out of his car, low to the ground like an alley-cat and aimed his pistol one more time at the front windows to the left of the PIU main doors. "Just to let you know I'm here, Paradise," he whispered before pulling the trigger. Shattered glass everywhere. Meat was on high alert and in his glory. Never complain, never explain. Oh, he would enjoy taking this little bitch down. Paradise would be begging him to let her lead the way to her brother before he was finished with her.

Meat hated making small talk en route to a kill and he was glad to be on his own today. In the time it took him to drive the 401 to Port Hope he had it all figured out. This would be easy compared to all he had endured to get the notches he had on his belt today. He was proud of every notch and he remembered every sordid detail. With pride.

What the hell would it take to turn a nun into a PI? Meat figured he had a couple seconds to let his mind wander. Whoever was inside with Paradise was probably an amateur PI at best. He figured Paradise was enjoying her little overnight visit with her new friend given that she was a girl and he was a boy. He smiled at the thought of them waking up to the sound of gun fire. Meat was anxious to make the bastard regret the day he ever met Paradise.

Meat made a mental note – *If there's more than one shooter I'll take them both out. My men will pay the price later for not giving me accurate information if that's the case. In particular, if the little nun can shoot a gun I should have had that information before leaving Toronto.*

He would soon find out.

51

Jim was down.

Clint was on his feet but injured.

Paradise was shaken but not hit.

Drawing her gun and adopting her locked-and-loaded stance Paradise was on high alert. Jim created a noise that drew attention to the front of the building where the windows had been shattered. Clint and Paradise rounded the outside of the building from the back. "Paradise, it's Meat so be extra careful," warned Clint. "I know it's him and we both know it's you he's after."

Meat saw a shadow inside the building and fired again as he slowly moved closer, gun solidly on the shadow.

"Paradise, is that you hiding in there like a little girl? Get off your ass and get out here. I'd say fight like a man but it's you we're talking about." This was a first Meat thought. He had never battled it out with a damn nun before. How hard could it be? He couldn't wait to get his hands, and his gun, on her.

Meat was blind-sided as Paradise approached to his left. He felt a gun pressed against the middle of his back before he heard her voice. "Drop the gun Meat. *Drop it.*" He knew he could reach for his second gun if he could distract her. "I said, drop it."

Impressive he thought. Score one for her. "You got me. Don't shoot. Please don't shoot me." Meat dropped his gun. He did *not* put his hands in the air.

He's not that mean after all, Paradise thought. And he seems more than a bit afraid. For a second Paradise forgot exactly who she was dealing with. Her inexperience was showing and she let her guard down. She lost her focus.

One split second was all it took.

With killer precision and speed Meat had his second gun in hand and with a swift kick he disarmed Paradise and took her to the ground. "You didn't actually think I'd come here with a single gun now did you, Miss Private Eye? It's y*ou,* Paradise, I assume." He held her firmly beneath him and placed his gun between her eyes. "Well I'm pleased to make your acquaintance." The sneer Paradise saw on his face was almost as eerie as the cold tip of his gun. Meat was enjoying this. He continued to bark at her.

"Listen up you, pretty young thing. And you *are* a pretty young thing. Tell me where your brother is, Paradise, or I swear I'll blow your head off. You won't be so attractive with your head missing – so speak now or forever hold your peace as they say. In my world we say, 'Forever hold your *piece'* too but we spell it differently." Meat was enjoying his own humour.

Paradise was surprisingly calm. "You're the one who had Wilmot. Tell me what you did with my brother. Tell me where Wilmot is." If the end was near she needed to know every detail surrounding her brother's disappearance, and Marie's too, before meeting her death. If Clint was close enough to hear, he'd be able to share the information with her parents if she didn't survive.

"That's right. I'm getting ahead of myself. I can't blow your head off just yet. You get to live at least until we have a nice long talk about that sneaky brother of yours. I have a score to settle with Wilmot. He didn't do what he was told."

"And what was that exactly?"

"You wouldn't know this, Paradise, but there're many ways to make money. I built my gang from the ground up. We brought your brother on board for a specific reason. I'll call it *babysitting*. Wilmot's job was to pick up and deliver the little bundles of joy to me. He sold drugs for us when babies weren't dropping if you follow me. It wasn't rocket science. He should have been able to follow orders."

"And he did that, I assume?"

"Yes and no. He was a natural but he proved to be dishonest. Your big brother bought and sold well enough but he tried to keep a bit of my money. *My money*. He wanted it for himself and his little idiot-brained girlfriend. Do you know *Lady* Marie, Paradise? Wilmot

247

called her his lady. Made me sick. I'm looking for her too."

"Marie? Yes I do know her. I like her very much. I'm looking for Marie as well as my brother so don't pretend it's me who knows where they are."

"Stupid bitch. You're as stupid as your low-life brother. You and Marie probably have about the same brainpower come to think of it. Now let's get down to business. Where. Are. They?"

"Low-life? Did you call Wilmot low-life? What does that make you?" Paradise tried to move her head away from the gun but Meat only pressed it harder against the side of her face.

"You're actually quite a looker. I didn't figure you for pretty or with any figure at all to be honest but I can see and I can feel your body under me. Not bad. Not bad at all. Maybe I won't kill you just yet." Meat pressed his body harder against Paradise. It was getting difficult for her to breath.

Again Paradise tried to dislodge his body from hers and Meat was loving it. "Don't make me pull the trigger before you get all of your answers. I've got the upper hand here. Remember that. Now, any more questions?"

"You beat Marie into submission. I saw the bruises. I asked her if it was you but she didn't want to give you up. Or, she was frightened to cross you. Is that why you almost killed her? Because she dared to cross you? That must have made you feel like a big strong man. I think

Marie weighs under a hundred pounds compared to your three hundred or so."

"Oh, Paradise, you've got it all wrong. Especially on that last night I saw Wilmot. I was busy kicking the shit out of your brother and had to dispatch one of my men to *speak* with Marie. I sent him there to do more than beat her. He was supposed to *kill her*."

Paradise was only half-listening. She could see Clint out of the corner of her eye. He was trying to close the gap between himself and Meat. Clint was bleeding from the face and head – likely from the shattered glass following the gun blast through the windows. His gun was pointed directly at Meat but he was moving slowly.

Clint wondered why Paradise was being so aggressive with Meat. Clearly she *did not* have the upper hand yet she spoke with confidence he didn't quite understand.

Trying to keep Meat talking Paradise kept pressing, or trying to. "I'll forget about Marie if you'll tell me where my brother is. Please take me to Wilmot and deal with us both together." She would figure out next steps later.

Laughing out loud now Meat began to lose his concentration. Paradise could see him lighten up. He was comfortable in the moment.

"Well, look at you saying please. That'll carry a lot of weight, Paradise. *Let her go because she said please.* Not my style, darlin.' Time for some answers I think,"

x

Meat said as he attempted to grind against her body beneath him one more time.

Enjoying the sound of his own voice Meat continued. "What the hell were you doing in a convent in the first place? I have to wonder what was going on in your head. Did your parents force you to go? You're a bit of a mystery, I guess. Hey, I bet I've got myself a little virgin here. Isn't that right, Paradise? Did anyone give it to you before you put on those ugly black clothes and slept with God? Sleeping with me would be sleeping with *a* god. Oh girl, I've got a new plan for you." Meat knew he was focused on the wrong thing. Hot young women did that to him.

If he only knew, thought Paradise. "What an ass you are, Meat. Or should I call you Mr. Meat? You make my skin crawl."

Clint was unsure where Paradise would go next with her line of questioning. She was making him even more nervous than he was already. He had to make his move before she got them both killed or at the very least got herself killed.

Seeing the rage in Meat's eyes Paradise knew she had gone too far. She couldn't move under the weight of his body. He was sitting on her chest now but at least his gun was no longer firmly pressed between her eyes. Meat seemed to be considering his options and he allowed the gun to move from her face to the air and back again. At the moment the gun was pressed against her cheek, or was it her ear? The weight of his bulk was causing severe breathing issues for Paradise and she struggled to keep a clear head. She knew Clint was trying to get to her.

Less than an instant later Paradise, Jim, Clint and Meat all heard the police cruisers in the distance. Inside and away from the gunfire Jim had been able to reach the phone and call for help.

Meat knew he had to return to his car and get out of the area before the police got any closer. He had to end her life her now. As much as he was enjoying playing with her mind, and her body, time was running out for little Miss PI.

As Meat pulled the trigger to kill Paradise there was a second trigger pull just behind him. In precisely the same fraction of a second two clear shots rang out.

Bang.

Bang.

Epilogue

Three weeks later.

"Ladies and gentlemen, this is your Captain, Doreen Foss, speaking. I neglected to inform you, our flying time to Honolulu will be nine hours and forty-five minutes. Sit back and relax. Meal service will begin shortly."

Paradise used the flight time to update her list of things to do when she returned to Toronto and then to Cape St Mary. Making lists still brought calm and if she ever needed calm it was now.

1. *Thomas.* I'll give myself time to get to know Thomas all over again. This time, we're two mature adults. I understand he has a family because his mother told me so. The fact that I'm still in love with Thomas is a problem. It's my problem – best kept to myself.

2. *Wilmot.* His name doesn't need to be on any list. My brother is always first on my mind when I wake up each morning. I'm certain Thomas has some news about him. Why else would he be so insistent I fly to Honolulu? I'm hoping Wilmot is actually there *with* Thomas. That would be ideal. Ideal but unlikely.

3. *Mom and Dad.* I vow to spend quality time with Mom and Dad prior to relocating. Dad and I would be

comfortable at the shooting range while Mom and I would be comfortable anywhere.

4. *Pops.* Speak with Pops when I get to the Cape. I owe him answers and I need to talk with Pops about a number of things. Living arrangements in particular. Pops' home is old and rundown *and* I love it. A strong character is present in every corner. I'm going to ask if Pops will sell it to me. We could restore it together. I know money is tight for Pops and this way we would both win, and we would be together. The mismatched recliner and threadbare sofas are things we could live with while we tackle red clay roof tiles that fly off with every windstorm. The not-so-white stucco walls need attending to and the old oak tongue and groove begs for some tender love and care. I have only been inside Pops' home a few times but from the outside it is beyond beautiful.

5. *Elise.* Find Elise and ask if she can tell me about my birth mother. I would love to hear about my mom from a woman's prospective. From her friend. Additionally, how well did Elise know my father? Did she know my birth parents *before* they moved in with Pops and got married? Other than driving the get-away car what other role did she play in my adoption? Elise could, hopefully, answer many of my questions.

6. *Marie.* Find her. Help her. Get to know her.

7. *Pd – Private Investigator.* Wrap up my many jobs and focus on my chosen career.

8. *Infants born at the convent.* I don't know how to go about this one but I know it has to be on my list. I need

facts and right now I have none. I can't wrongfully accuse anyone but at the same time I can't let it go. I lived at the convent for five years and I have to think I would've known if anything illegal was going on. Wouldn't I? The more time that passes, the more I am unsure what I remember correctly.

9. *Cape St Mary.* Develop a timeline for returning to Cape St Mary on a more permanent basis. This will include a plan for my mother to visit. I want Mom to know how big a part of my life she is and making plans with her before I move will please her.

10. *Morning Glory and Dawn.* Bottom of my list and to be honest I might not get to this one. I can't do everything (even though I sometimes think I can). The girls may have to make their own decisions and live with them. Hopefully they will make better decisions in the future than they have made thus far. Because they were my first case I can't forget them.

11. ~~Hair and wardrobe.~~ This was such a personal but huge item on my list. I just need to cross it off one more time! As I visit the washroom on board and prepare for touchdown in Honolulu I'm glad my hair has been cut and I finally have some *new* clothes. Frenchy's is great but my new clothes fit me so well and add to my confidence in ways I can't explain. Didn't get those killer high heeled shoes but they'll show up in my closet one day soon. Maybe I'll find them in Hawaii.

***

Her parents had been surprisingly supportive of Paradise making a sudden trip to Hawaii. Her mother in particular hugged Paradise tightly as she whispered in her ear, "I know in my heart of hearts this is going to work out for you, Paradise. You go and find Thomas and you get your answers. This is about *you dear*."

Even her father wished her well and asked her to come back *soon*. Paradise knew it was a stretch for him to be so personal. He was trying. Ben was extremely proud of his PI daughter and had told her so.

During the Port Hope shoot-out, the monster known as Meat Cove died instantly from a single gunshot wound to the head. Clint fired the fatal shot. Sadly Meat took with him whatever information he had about Wilmot and Marie.

Paradise escaped with her life. The bullet fired from Meat's gun grazed the side of her head. When twenty-three stitches were removed, the day prior to her departure, Paradise was left with a very long scar through her hairline and on the left side of her face. Her face had been black and blue compliments of Meat. For the most part, the bruises had disappeared. Those she brought with her, Paradise hoped were hidden by makeup and clothing.

Clint and Jim were healing well and after advising Paradise she might want to work on her interrogation skills (Don't interrogate someone who has a gun pointed at your head, for example.) they gave her some space.

Clint called just before Paradise left her parents' home for the airport. He offered her a job with PIU and suggested she update her resume to add their recent take down of a well-known criminal. He reinforced the job offer before hanging up but this time he added he would need the approval of his two partners. He didn't think there would be a problem. Paradise thanked Clint for everything, including the fact that he had brought the first smile to her lips in days.

Paradise could only wonder what her future held as the plane touched down in Honolulu almost ten hours after take off.

***

Less than two minutes after she stepped off the plane Paradise saw him. *Her Thomas.* If it was possible he was even more handsome than she remembered. She was shaking and feared she might faint. She didn't.

They approached each other tentatively. It was hard to believe this day had arrived. Paradise felt she was in a crossword puzzle looking for that eleven-across-word but not able to find it. Speechless.

As Thomas reached her, almost in slow-motion, a little girl appeared from behind him. She was holding his hand tightly but looking directly at Paradise. Thomas was trying to keep her out of sight but that was clearly not going to happen. As he looked down Paradise heard him whisper to the child, "We talked about this remember?

I'll introduce you in a few seconds. Okay?" Not okay, she definitely wasn't going to hide and continued to step away from Thomas and into her own space.

For the first time in her life, Paradise was looking at a mirror image of herself. Her own face was staring back at her. Her eyes. Her smile. Her hair. Her height at such a young age.

A fast calculation of the number of years since she had given birth in the convent and Paradise knew it was possible. *This was actually possible.* This little girl…

Without waiting for a proper introduction her mirror image stepped forward. "Aloha, Paradise, my name is Hope d'Entremont-Adams."

Hope looked up at her father and saw the frown on his face. Thomas smiled in spite of what was happening. He would share later that Hope talks too fast and everything runs into one single sentence when she's nervous – just like her mother. Thomas tried to take control of the conversation but his daughter beat him to it. Again.

Hope knew this was not how they practised meeting Paradise. She didn't care. Anyway, it was too late now so she decided to keep going.

With a full-on hug she continued in a whisper, "Daddy told me who you are. Do you know who I am? I'm not supposed to say anything yet but I am so excited. Do you know? *Do you?*"

Hope couldn't contain her excitement. "Daddy said you're very smart and he also said you would know the second you saw me. Is it true?" The young girl's mind was racing. "I do look like you don't you think?

Paradise let her mind drift back to the eve of her sixteenth birthday. They met at their secret place. Thomas told her he loved her and wanted to marry her. He asked her to concentrate on finishing high school and, at the same time, he would graduate from the RCMP academy and start earning real money. He would be able to support his wife. As Paradise began to speak that evening so many years ago, she watched the depth of his eyes change from surprise, to anger to sadness. She told Thomas she had made a life altering decision – at sixteen. She chose *Him* over *him*. Thomas turned and walked away without another word. She knew he understood her decision. He just didn't accept it. She hadn't seen Thomas again. Until today.

Thomas and Paradise had yet to speak a word to each other. Hope, watching intently, was confused when she finally heard them speak. She would ask for an explanation later.

In unison, Hope heard her parents say, "Save the Last Dance for Me."